TROUBLE WITH
EXPLOSIVES

TROUBLE WITH EXPLOSIVES

by SALLY KELLEY

cover by Gloria Kamen

SCHOLASTIC BOOK SERVICES

NEW YORK • TORONTO • LONDON • AUCKLAND • SYDNEY • TOKYO

For my sons, Charles and Kenan

Copyright © 1976 by Sally Kelley. All rights reserved. This edition is published by Scholastic Book Services, a division of Scholastic Magazines, Inc., 50 West 44th Street, New York, NY 10036, by arrangement with Bradbury Press, Inc.

12 11 10 9 8 7 6 5 4 3 2 1   3   8 9/7 0 1 2 3/8

Contents

P...P...P...Polly

My name is Polly Banks.

That sounds easy to say. Right?

Wrong. I stutter.

Last year if I said, "My name is Polly Banks," I sounded like a car starting up with a bad engine. "M...M...M...My name is P...P...P...Polly B...B...B...Banks."

This is the story of how I stopped sounding like a car. It, the cure, has something to do with the Pledge of Allegiance, a psychiatrist named Andrea Maxie, a girl named Sis Hawkins and a teacher who got shrunk.

I was eleven when we moved for the umpteenth time in six years to Atlanta, Georgia. That was a year ago.

My father was a rising young executive. He traveled and rose, traveled and rose. He is in plastics, and my mother was one more organized woman. She saved boxes from move to move and put them in the basement in a box labeled BOXES.

We leased a home in Happy Valley, a suburb of Atlanta. The houses were set back on wide green lawns, and almost everyone had a snarling dog on a chain in the rear. (My friend Sis Hawkins told me there were a lot of scared people in Happy Valley.)

We landed on Thursday, January 2. By the next Monday, the curtains were up, the dishes were stacked neatly in the kitchen cabinets, and I had an appointment with a new shrink on January 15.

Don't get me wrong. My parents love me. They just didn't understand stuttering — nobody had ever stuttered in my family before.

My Uncle Harry used to drink too much.

My mom said he'd been to Alcoholics Anonymous, and they had cured him.

I asked her if they had Stutterers Anonymous, and she said, "That's not funny."

I also had an appointment at a new school, which my mother found in an ad before we moved. "Mandalay for Happy Boys and Girls."

That Monday morning I had on my mother's best outfit — she picked out all my clothes in those days. My dark blue dress with a white collar hung neatly over my knee socks and brown loafers. My hair was braided so tightly I had a headache.

You may ask, "Why didn't you tell your mother not to braid your hair so tight?"

I reply, "Do you know how hard it is to say 'Stop that!' when you stutter?"

Besides, I hated the look on my mother's face when I stammered. I know she tried, but as I strained to get it out, I could see her face squinch up in pain. If I had been sticking her with pins, it would have hurt less.

Better to have a headache.

We arrived at Mandalay. The buildings were similar to the houses, big with stone walls and high arches.

I followed my mother into the school office. She is a very beautiful woman, tall and athletic. She heads drives and speaks up in public meetings.

The principal, Miss Heartbang, was standing just inside the door at the front desk. Seeing us walk in, "New Pupil" written all over me, Miss Heartbang sighed happily and smiled.

Then it happened.

My mother said, "Polly, will you wait here a moment. I have to have a little talk with Miss Heartbang."

I sat in the reception room, trying not to think of all the scary things ahead. When you stutter, move around a lot, and have to face new schools, new teachers, and strange, regular kids each year, the First Day gets worse and worse.

My mother disappeared into a smaller office with the principal. The door shut.

I started to count slowly. The last "little talk" had lasted to 300. That principal was slow. Miss Heartbang must have been sharp; I was at 150 when the door opened, and I knew "Polly's little problem" had been revealed.

Miss Heartbang was not smiling. "Well . . . Well . . . Well . . ." she said.

I said goodbye to my mother, and Miss Heartbang led me down the hall to the fifth-grade class of Miss Patterson.

I knew trouble was ahead — P is not my best letter.

Miss Heartbang opened the door and we stepped in.

4

A tiny woman, so skinny her hands would slice ham, was bending over this girl and shaking her fist in the girl's face.

I could see books littering the floor by the girl's desk; some were sprawled open like they had just been dropped.

The woman was screaming, "Sis Hawkins, you are the most unmanageable child in the whole class."

Now, when you don't talk you learn a lot from people's expressions. I had to catch my breath, because the girl was grinning as if the cussing-out was some kind of joke. Her eyes were wide, not beaten, maybe a little bored.

Her face was round, and her hair was a mass of black curls. She was as immature as me, you know, bottlecaps.

"Yoo hoo, Miss Patterson," Miss Heartbang interrupted.

The skinny teacher turned, and I swear, as I watched she gained ten pounds. I mean, she got round and soft, and her smile would have cooked chicken.

"Miss Heartbang," she cooed. "I didn't hear you come in."

"I've brought you a nice new pupil," Miss Heartbang said, pointing at me.

And as seventeen pairs of eyes switched

from Miss Patterson and the girl to me, I heard Miss Heartbang say, "I have to rush off. I know you'll take care of things."

Miss Patterson said, "Of course."

The door shut.

Then I wanted to run away, because Miss Patterson tiptoed toward me, and I felt her hand on my headache, her breath on my cheek as she leaned over. Then I heard those words, those terrible words, "And what is our new little pupil's name?"

I took a deep breath. I tried to think of all the advice I had had all my stuttering years — don't get nervous; trust yourself; remember, it doesn't matter.

I opened my mouth.

"P...P...P...P...P...P...P...P...P...P...P...P..."

I had to take another breath. "P...P...P... P...P..."

My hands grew cold. My face got red. I heard chairs squeaking, giggles rising. I continued my terrible, "P...P..."

Then, through the haze, I heard a girl's voice. "Miss Patterson, I gotta go to the bathroom."

The black-haired girl was jumping up and down like a dancer. "I mean I really gotta go," she yelled.

Miss Patterson pounced on her like a tiger, grabbing her arm. "I can't take much more of this behavior . . ." she began, then she released the girl. "You're excused," she snapped.

The girl was out of the room in a jiffy.

To my amazement, I said loud and clear, "Polly Banks. My name is Polly Banks."

When the class settled down, I was shown to my desk.

The black-haired girl returned. I smiled gratefully.

She stuck out her tongue.

Sports

At recess you'd have thought I was invisible.

I take that back. A fat girl named May Biggs (honestly, Biggs!) invited me to share a snack, half a chocolate cake.

She was a freak, I could tell, and I know all about freaks — kids who are too fat, too smart, kids with an out-to-lunch look.

(Freakdom changes. Maybe somebody should put out a monthly magazine on Freaks so we can keep up. One thing never changes. Stutterers are freaks.)

I shook my head at May Biggs. I thought I was free, but another girl walked toward me. Her name was Sarah Coots, I discovered later.

8

You know in the movies how criminals walk as if a cop was behind them? That was the way Sarah Coots walked, looking over her shoulder. She had her hand in her coat pocket, and I swear, it looked like she was carrying a gun.

I ran away. Freaky!

The class had gathered at the flagpole. Sis was organizing them into team sports.

I thought of my mother as I wandered over.

"Let's play soccer," someone yelled.

"Basketball!"

"Let's play nothing."

Sis shouted loudest of all. "Okay, we'll play kickball. I'm captain."

Right then, I knew I wanted to play on Sis's team; she had the look of a winner.

The other captain was Gordon Morgan.

(He's really a neat kid. He's going to be a professional football player, and I'm going to watch every game.)

We ambled toward the playing field. I straggled behind.

The school was perched on a hill. A long flight of steps carried you down the steep gravely bank to the kickball diamond, then the ground dropped away again to a creek that in winter was rutty with frozen mud.

By the time I arrived at the foot of the steps, everyone but Sis and Gordon had lined up to be selected for teams. There were sixteen playing; it took six and one half picks to get down to three, May Biggs, me and a skinny boy named Rob Peters who was still nine and one grade ahead — a freak.

Sis sighed, "I'll take May."

"Get on over," Gordon said to Rob.

Sis motioned to me. "Okay, what's-your-name. Get behind me."

The class giggled; my spirits sank.

Maybe I won't have to prove anything, I thought briefly.

Gordon's team was up first. Our team was out in field. Sis was pitcher, and my deskmate, Cynthia Feingold, was the first baseman. My spot was in left field.

Gordon kicked a home run.

Three high flies; they were out.

We were in.

Sis lined us up. I was kicking after her. Boom! Boom! Boom! Three flies. Our team was out almost before we were in.

I was getting nervous in left field. May was next to me at center whining like a four-year-old about how hungry she was.

One runner was caught on first, another on second. Sis snagged a pop-up foul.

The score: 1 to 0.

When we walked in to be up, I could tell Sis hated to lose.

Our first player was out on the first kick.

It was Sis's turn. She squared her shoulders and moved into the kicker's box like she was a pro. She wasn't smiling or anything.

Gordon paused to think.

Quickly, he pulled his hand back and sent the ball wobbling down the worn path; Sis ran to meet it.

It was a good one.

Splat!

The ball took off low and fast past second base. Nobody could catch it as a fly. Sis ran like the devil was after her. I thought it would be a home run, but the other team was good.

She was stopped at third.

I was next.

My head buzzed with my chance . . . good impression . . . no freak . . .

I felt numb.

The field was quiet, waiting. I stepped into the kicker's box.

I could see Gordon was wondering whether to be kind to the "poor thing" or to play it straight. He made up his mind, and fell into his pitcher's stance; it was going to be straight. That's when I began to admire him. He was like Sis, tough but fair.

I braced myself to start my run. I took one last look at the place I wanted the ball to go — right over Rob Peters' head.

Then things sort of blur over. I remember running to meet the ball, pulling my leg back. I closed my eyes to concentrate. I felt the rubber ball slap against my foot, and the impact run up my leg.

Whatever I had done was done.

When I looked, the ball had risen so high it seemed it would hit the school. Up, up it soared toward the big bank, past Rob Peters' outstretched hands, bouncing against the gravel and rolling back slowly, like it had all the time in the world.

I had it made.

The trip around the bases was too quick to enjoy. I only remember the shouts from my team.

Sis came in first, then I followed.

The score: 2 to 1, we were the winners.

Kids were hitting me, you know like they do to congratulate you. But it was over in a flash. The bell rang; recess was done.

Sis stayed to walk me up the steps. She didn't say anything until we got to the flagpole. Then she cocked her head and gave me a you-ain't-so-freaky-after-all look.

"Your mouth doesn't work worth a plugged nickel," she said. "But your foot is fine."

"D...D...D...Darn right," I said.

"D...D...D...Darn right," she mocked me.

For some reason, I laughed.

But when I returned to the room, everything was the same. I had had good "first days" before, but nothing ever came of them. I still stuttered.

Miss Patterson

The first week of school passed quickly.
Moving does that. Things are out of focus until you know where the bathrooms are, what
teachers are like, who's smart and knows it,
who's dumb and doesn't know it. I had the
class sized up quickly. Four were out-and-out
freaks, Rob, May, Sarah and me. Three were
absolutely non-freaks, Cynthia Feingold, Sis
and Gordon. That left ten who were freaky
sometimes and non-freaky other times. Five
boys were regular on the playing field and
crazy in class; five girls combed their hair
when they weren't giggling, which was most
of the time.

The teachers had their quirks too. Miss
Holmes, the P.E. teacher talked so tough I

was scared of her. But Sis Hawkins said, "Marshmallow."

It was true. Miss Holmes always rushed up to the losers and tried to make them feel better; one time she cried when a nasty little kid got licked in a fair fight.

The first, third, and sixth-grade teachers were drabbies.

Only the second-grade teacher, Miss Tillstrom, was something else. She was a little eager person. She had a small boa constrictor in a glass cage in her classroom so the little kids could watch it grow. And she didn't care how many times the kids fed the goldfish. (No fish ever died. Smart fish!)

"Dynamite," Sis Hawkins said.

It was funny to watch Miss Tillstrom at lunch; she always sat and ate with Miss Patterson. They were friends, old stiffneck Patterson and that cool teacher.

I guess Miss Tillstrom liked to play with boa constrictors too.

I knew immediately Miss Patterson was a bad one. I have had lazy teachers who rush out of the room every half hour to smoke. I had a third-grade teacher, Miss Wallingford, who slept behind her dark glasses while we did our silent reading. But, Miss Patterson was alert-mean.

I'd better describe the room because it could only belong to her. Everything was so in place, I thought my dad could have it plasticized.

We had table desks, six of them, three kids to each. I sat in the back row; Sis sat next to the flags and under Miss Patterson's eyes.

The walls were covered with pictures of George Washington, Robert E. Lee, Jefferson Davis, Stonewall Jackson, and three men I had never seen before. They looked like they had swallowed sour pickles. Sis said they were former Governors of Georgia. A large picture of Stone Mountain with its Civil War Riders decorated the coatroom door. A map of the Confederacy held up one wall, a map of Georgia the other. A large Confederate flag, a Georgia flag, and an American flag were to the side.

Our day started like this. First we'd line up outside and wait. Miss Patterson would come to the door like a general who had the battle plan ready for the day's fight.

"Children," she'd say. "Spit out your gum. Wipe your feet. Hands to your sides. March like soldiers. One. Two. Three. Take your seats."

I learned not to jostle anyone in line or act silly. Miss Patterson kept you in for nothing.

Mean as thunder.

She paused a moment, smiling as everyone quickly and quietly put their jackets in the coatroom. Miss Patterson always smiled, even if kids acted bad and she was saying mean things like, "Stay in" or "You failed the test." Her smile was cold and it gave me the weebie jeebies from the first day.

Each morning there was the roll call, then we would sit like holes punched in a computer card until Miss Patterson was satisfied. Then she would close the door.

(Sis said things had to be done the "Patterson Way" or not at all.)

Finally, and it always seemed an hour had passed, Miss Patterson would say, "Now!"

The first time, I snickered, it was so funny. Three kids rose. Cynthia stepped on my foot to hush me.

A needle hit a record. The tune was familiar, "Dixie" played by the Boston Pops.

Suddenly from out of the coatroom doorway stepped the three kids now changed into something looking like pictures you see around the Fourth of July — three men marching. One kid had on a three-cornered hat— he was the American Flag Kid. The Georgia Flag Kid had a plastic magnolia pinned on his shirt; the Confederate Kid wore a gray coat that, I swear, looked like it had a blood stain over the heart.

They marched twice around the room serious as beagles and everyone jumped up and stood at attention.

Nobody moved. Nobody smiled. Nothing.

The three kids trudged back into the coatroom. The music stopped. The flags were replaced in the stands.

Miss Patterson looked like she had swallowed the same thing as the Governors of Georgia.

The three took their seats and Miss Patterson said, "May Biggs, the Pledge."

We all joined in; I pretended to speak.

"I pledge allegiance to the Flag of the United States of America and to the Republic for which it stands, one Nation under God, indivisible, with liberty and justice for all."

May sat down; a half hour was shot. The "Patterson Way" never varied. Math was always at 9:31, Language Arts at 10:18, recess, Geography, lunch. I have to say that Miss Patterson was good, and fair, with Language Arts and Math. But after lunch, we had History. You guessed it, Southern History.

(Now me being from the North, I didn't

get all the Southern bit, but Sis said some Southerners have one eye on the past because it looks better than the present.)

Miss Patterson had a real hang-up. On and on she'd go. I didn't understand half of what she said. The more bored we got, chairs squeaking, kids coughing, kids rest-rooming it, the dreamier it made Miss Patterson.

Friday of the first week was really squirmy. I wanted to get out of there.

Miss Patterson called on Rob Peters. "Who was the State of Georgia named for?"

Rob had risen and stood beside his desk looking even younger than he was. He was nervous; History is not his best subject.

"George Washington," he said hopefully.

Somebody giggled. Miss Patterson turned so quickly the kids sitting at the desk near her jerked backwards as if she had smacked them.

"Georgia Washington?" Rob tried again.

"Was that his sister?" Miss Patterson said.

Now, I've noticed if you don't feel too sure of yourself, like being in a room full of kids two years older than you, sarcasm from a teacher is no help.

"Go on," Miss Patterson said. "Who was the State of Georgia named for?"

"I don't know," Rob moaned.

"You don't know!" Miss Patterson reared back and addressed the class. "What do you think of our smart little genius now, class?"

Rob stood so forlornly I thought he would topple over.

Miss Patterson had begun to glide slowly around the room like a panther on the prowl. I was unprepared.

"Polly Banks," she said, "who was the State of Georgia named for?"

I stood. I didn't know anything about the South except from a Black History course I'd had in Seattle.

"Well?" Miss Patterson said.

I had to say something.

"G...G...G...G...George Wallace?"

I heard someone giggle; I think it was Sis.

Miss Patterson snorted, "Georgia was a state one hundred years before George Wallace was born."

I had begun to clasp and unclasp my hands helplessly.

Miss Patterson's voice was raw. "Polly, who was the State . . ."

Before she could finish, Gordon had risen in the back. He pointed to the map of Georgia; there were facts written on the side. He spoke low like a preacher. "It says there Georgia was named for King George II of England." He looked at Rob. "I can see from where I sit, but Rob and Polly can't. It's not in the history books anywhere."

Miss Patterson crossed her arms like she was mad, then she smiled, not a good smile either, but one that made me think of false-teeth advertisements on TV — fakey.

She looked past Gordon like he wasn't there and said, "That will do."

We all sat down as Miss Patterson returned to her desk. She began reading a dull old document I couldn't understand.

School was out soon, and I tried to forget about it.

I had felt humiliated by teachers before.

Sis Hawkins

We lived over a mile from school. "The walk will do Polly good," my mother had said. I would have yelled "Hooray!" if I could, because nothing makes you feel more like you belong to a spot than walking home from school. As it was, I just smiled.

On the next Wednesday, school was over, a final "Dixie" had been sung, and I was heading home, happy to be away from Miss Patterson.

I was tired. I had played basketball at recess until I thought I'd drop. (I was top scorer.) Then, I had watched Miss Patterson fuss for fifteen minutes at Sis because Sis's desk was disorganized and messy. Even listening to a cussing-out can make you weary.

Three blocks away from school, I was feeling better. I had stopped to look around (Happy Valley still held surprises), when I felt a slap on my back so hard I dropped my books. I was mad.

"Hi," Sis said.

I nodded. I couldn't trust a "Hi."

Sis grabbed my books and pushed them into my hands. We stared at each other, then she started jumping up and down like a fighter. "Where are you going?" she said, stopping the bouncing and looking me square in the eyes.

I had to answer.

"T...T...T...T...T...T..." Sis cocked her head in mild curiosity. Then, slowly as I was still T-ing it, she reached up and put her finger up her nose.

"Hey," I yelled, "you aren't supposed to do that! You can't pick buggers in public!"

She shrugged her shoulders and went after the other nostril. "Who says?" she said.

"Everyone says, starting with my mother!"

Sis looked puzzled, and, as I paused for breath, she began to giggle.

"Why are you giggling?" I said.

"I w...w...w...wonder," she said.

I had been talking straight. It embarrassed me so much, I turned away quickly. My mind was crowded with questions. Did she think I had been putting on?

But, when I turned around and saw Sis hadn't left, I could only stutter, "S...S...S... S...S...S..."

Sis curled her little finger like she was drinking tea, then put her index finger up her nose. As if that wasn't enough, she put the finger of the other hand in her ear. She stuck out her tongue and looked cross-eyed.

Something must have clicked over in my throat, for when I stopped laughing, my stuttering was gone again. "Sis Hawkins, you are something else!"

She slapped me on the back and squealed, "Can't catch me!"

We ran until our breath was hot, then we walked slowly. Four blocks from my house, I had told her where I had moved from, how many times I had moved, what my parents' names were, what my mom and dad did — everything that had to be gotten out of the way for friends to be friends.

She was a good listener, not worrying at all when things were hard to get out.

When I started talking about my hiking, I knew I was trying to impress her.

"I'll t...t...t...tell you something, the greatest thing is hiking up mountains, gi...gi...gi...giant mountains." I paused. "You ever been h...h...h...hiking up a mountain?" I could see she hadn't.

Sis's eyes were as big as bubblegum. "You've been up a mountain?"

"With b...b...b...back p...p...p...p...packs and everything."

"How many times?"

"Every weekend, almost," I said. "One day I hiked nine m...m...m...miles with a twenty p...p...pound pack."

"Ever sleep outside in the woods?"

"Man, did I ever sleep outside in the woods! I b...b...b...b...bet I've slept outside a million times." Sis shook her head. "Maybe twenty," I corrected.

"I'd sure like that," Sis said.

"Don't you ever sleep outside?"

"South has too many snakes."

We walked silently.

"M...M...M...Maybe," I said. "If we ever go b...b...back, you could c...c...c...come too."

"You mean it?"

"I m...m...m...mean it."

"Tell me again about those mountains."

The last two blocks I gave it to her about hiking in the wilderness. I laid it on pretty thick about rock slides and dangerous cliffs, but — I don't know why — I couldn't tell her about the elk.

By the time we reached my house, we were silent; the mountain stuff had run out. Sis looked like it was her turn to tell what was important.

I started for the driveway, when Sis grabbed my arm. She was really serious. "Miss Patterson is a tyrant," she said. "She's sick."

"She looks healthy as a h...h...h...horse to me," I said.

"She's sick inside her head."

I wanted to smile at the thought of Sis looking inside Miss Patterson through her open mouth. Instead, I said, "I d...d...don't understand."

"I read about it in my dad's . . . I mean a book," Sis continued. "Anybody who acts as she does, scaring people, has something wrong with his head. My mother said Hitler was a tyrant."

"G...G...Go on," I said.

"Doesn't matter."

"D...D...Does too." Sis still looked serious.

Just then my mother yelled from the door, "Hurry, Polly!" and I raced for the house.

I expected Sis to follow. When I looked back she was leaving. "See you tomorrow," she called and was gone.

My mother was full of business.

"What took you so long? We have to go to your psychiatrist's. We'll be late. What will she think?"

I surrendered my books. My face was scrubbed, and I was rushed to the car.

This was shrink day, and I had forgotten all about it. I sank back in the seat miserably. All the wonderful talk with Sis just faded away. I was a freak after all. Wasn't I going to a shrink?

Shrinks

Question: What is a shrink?

Answer: Choose one.

1. A four-legged animal who eats cabbage.
2. A machine down at the laundromat — a washer, a dryer, a shrink.
3. A psychiatrist.

If you chose number three you are right.

I got my first shrink in Seattle.

It all started on a mountain.

I can't remember a time in my life I didn't stammer a little. I've heard my mom say to my dad a zillion times, "Don't worry. She'll outgrow it."

"But, Elizabeth, it may hurt her chances in life," he'd reply.

"A little stuttering hurt a smart, pretty girl like Polly!" my mother would say, "Nonsense, you'd think it was dangerous."

When I was ten, two summers ago, we were hiking in the Olympic Mountains near Seattle. We'd been on the trail for three days and were twenty miles from anybody. I was loving it, going to sleep watching the stars, waking up to the sun shining through the mountain passes, eating breakfast that tasted of smoke, getting on the trail by 7:00. Perfect!

Each of us took turns walking first; nothing was scheduled.

By 5:00 that afternoon we were pooped.

The trail was winding between outcroppings of rock. I was in the lead; my mom and dad were ten or twenty steps behind, talking and giggling.

I was so happy, just watching my feet going up and down on the ground, I didn't notice at first the thing standing before me, but when I rounded a thick boulder, I almost bumped into a mother elk and her calf feeding in the twilight.

My heart dropped to my ankles seeing this big hunk of fur and face and antlers, three times as big as my dad or anybody, towering over me, mean-faced.

A moment passed as the elk sized up the situation. I watched her slowly lower her head and flick her ears back and forth as if she could shoo me away. I saw her calf skidder to her side for protection.

Then I knew I was in real trouble. I had opened my mouth to scream and nothing came out. No "Help!" No nothing.

All I could do was stammer, "D...D...D...D...D..."

I never worked so hard at anything.

The mama elk edged nearer, looking fiercer, like she wanted to toss me up in the air and over the mountains. I stood with my mouth open. I was shaking and weeping. The elk was so close I could feel her hot breath on my cheek.

"Crack!" exploded the air.

My dad had used his rifle, shooting it straight up.

The elk reared, turned and loped down the trail and out of sight, her calf right behind her.

I came close to fainting. My mother's arm caught me, then my father's. My mother was crying; my father was cursing. It was tender.

As my dad set up camp, I was shaking as if I had a chill. My voice was dead gone.

Slowly our nerves recovered, but nobody had much to say. During supper, I saw the worried looks pass between my mom and dad.

They must have thought I was asleep, but I overheard my mom crying in the dark. "She couldn't even call for help."

"We will have to do something," my dad said.

"Oh, Fred," my mom whimpered. "What did we do wrong?"

I felt like crying too, because I had made everybody so miserable. But my dad said in a voice so strong, so reassuring that my tears dried in my eyes, "Nobody did anything wrong. We'll just get it fixed. That's all. By heaven, she will be fine."

When we returned, my mom made an appointment with Dr. Daphne Fetlock.

Our first visit was on a gray Seattle afternoon. My mom had gotten nervouser and nervouser as the day came closer.

I didn't know what the doctor was going to do. I imagined there might be a switch in my throat somebody could adjust, like when a fuse blows out and you have to go to the basement and jiggle something.

We wound through trashy streets and parked in a circular garage that made me

dizzy. Out one building and in another; going
up in the elevator, my spirits went down.

We walked along a dark hall, then I saw
the door. Daphne Fetlock, M.D. (I knew what
"M.D." didn't say: Psychiatrist.)

I wanted to run away. Psychiatrists meant
crazy folks or drunks, like my Uncle Harry.

But my mom had my arm, and I was
ushered into the driest room I have ever seen;
lumpy furniture, bright lights, abstract pictures — when a mountain scene would have
been great.

Then I saw Dr. Fetlock.

Have you ever seen people who look like
animals? Dr. Fetlock looked like . . . *an elk!*
She was tall and her face was filled up with
a long nose and big teeth and thick glasses.
Her hair was arranged in two knots like two
small antlers. She walked flat-footed too.
Clump! Clump! Clump!

"You must be the Bankses?" she said too
loud.

I think my mother would have fallen into
the big woman's arms if she would have let
her. "Doctor Fetlock," she sighed.

We settled in Dr. Fetlock's inner office and
I watched my mother — who had organized
voter's drives, league meetings, and moved

us every year — unravel before me. Her talking was non-stop.

"I thought I'd call and get this appointment, because of our problem . . . On this mountain this elk . . . My husband is in plastics . . . I came from a small town in Ohio, Camp Coolidge . . ."

Dr. Fetlock leaned back and listened.

Once, she said, "Tell me about your parents."

My mother relaxed. She talked about her youth in Camp Coolidge and her father and mother.

It seemed strange, Dr. Fetlock and me sitting listening to my mother talk about her mother.

Then I understood. Dr. Fetlock didn't know who was the patient.

We had gotten off on the wrong foot.

But by the next meeting things were straightened out.

I went once a week for the three months we had left in Seattle.

Each time was like every other. I'd come in, and Dr. Fetlock would talk awhile, then I'd stutter for the rest of the hour.

Spit would fly.

Dr. Fetlock would say when my time was

up, "That's very good, Polly. See you next week."

I'll give her credit; she did try. The problem was she wanted to talk about the past, and I wanted to talk about the future — when would I stop moving? when would I stop stuttering? when would I stop being a freak?

She'd ask, "What were you doing last year?"

I'd give it to her so bad she'd have to get a Kleenex out and wipe off her glasses.

She took a lot of spit off me.

She must have told my mom and dad something, because I noticed they asked my opinion more. And for a while I tried to have opinions unsuccessfully. Then they began saying things like "This will be our last move" so I knew Dr. Fetlock was talking even if I wasn't.

I didn't believe my parents. (Sis says I'll always be spooked by a moving van.)

On our last meeting, I wanted to tell her that living in the past was not a too-cool thing to do. Instead, I just shook her hand.

I was stunned; her eyes watered.

Dr. Maxie

It took a half hour to drive from Happy Valley to my new shrink.

My mother chatted all the way; I only half-listened. I guess I was waiting for her to ask something important like "Who was that girl walking you home?" or "Do you like your hair in braids?"

But, to be fair, I never told her important things either, even after Dr. Fetlock said I should. So, driving along, my mom talked and I was silent.

I was surprised when we pulled off onto a quiet street. I was expecting another Fetlock office, but the building sat among a small woods. I walked slowly up the mossy steps and opened a red door. Inside, the rooms were soft and quiet, like our living room.

We had only time to say our names to the receptionist sitting at a corner desk when a small woman darted in like a busy butterfly and stopped before us.

She had long hair, and I remember watching her eyes, dark blue and so deep I thought of the lakes I had seen on top of the mountains.

My mother began. "I'm Mrs. Banks. This is Polly. You must be Dr. Maxie. We are sooooooo glad . . ."

The woman smiled at my mom patiently. "Yes," she said, then she turned to me not like I was something, but somebody.

I got out a "Hi!" with only six tries.

"Hi yourself," she said. "How about coming with me?" She motioned me down a hall with four doors on each side.

My mother started to follow, but Dr. Maxie's voice stopped her, not meanly, but with authority. "Polly will be out in about an hour."

I swear my mom said, "Yes ma'am."

As I walked down the hall, I began to feel different, like I was going into another world.

I can't explain it, but strange things happen in a shrink's office.

Dr. Maxie waited at the last door to let me in. I stood in the middle of the room, while she shut the door noiselessly and walked to the large window and sat in one of the two big chairs that looked into a small courtyard.

She had not said a word, no questions, no answers. She just sat there, smiling warmly, encouragingly, not like Miss Patterson.

She didn't motion me to sit, to stand, to stay, to leave, nothing. She looked at me; I looked back.

It was weird.

The silence was uncomfortable. I tried to think of something else. I inspected the room with my eyes. I gazed out the window trying not to look at the doctor.

I got mad. What was she waiting for? Why didn't she say something? She should have known I stuttered, that I was a freak.

Silence.

I don't know how long the contest lasted, but somehow I found myself in the other chair. I opened my mouth to speak and a funny thing happened. As I began to talk, tears ran down my cheeks.

"I d...d...d...d...don't want to s...s...s...s... stutter any more."

She leaned over slowly and spoke. "Then, we can begin our work." She cocked her head and winked. "Help yourself to some Kleenex first, Miss Polly Banks."

Surprise

The rest of the hour is hazy. As I cried, crazy things tumbled out, then I began to hiccup.

I was dead tired when Dr. Maxie stood up and said, "Our time is up."

At the door I turned to say goodbye.

Dr. Maxie was smiling. "You know it's not hopeless now, don't you," she said.

I must have nodded yes. But, as I walked down the hall, I repeated to myself, "It's not hopeless . . . it's not hopeless."

The ride home was solemn. My mom tried to make small talk. "Look at that cute little dog. You need anything from the drugstore?"

I tuned her out.

We ate supper alone; my dad was out of

town. I was so tired I could have napped in my mashed potatoes. My mom still talked. "What a nice night! Want some more milk? How about another piece of cake?"

After nodding yes, no, then no again, I said, "I got to go to b...b...b...bed."

My mom had on her suffering look. I knew she was going to say something embarrassing like, "I'm proud of you" or "I love you." Instead, she said, "Sweet dreams" and hugged me quick.

I hit the bed like a rocket, and that was that.

My mom's advice went out the window. I had wild dreams. I was on a big, wide range — you know, cowboy country. I was rounding up something that looked like elks, then I saw everything was backward. I was on top of an elk rounding up my mom and Dr. Fetlock. Everybody was miserable. It was a nightmare.

Fade out. Fade in. I was moving again. I was inside the new house and the moving van drove up. I ran to meet it. The doors flew open and a merry-go-round sounded in the distance, gay and cheerful. Standing inside were Sis Hawkins and Dr. Maxie. They jumped out and said, "Surprise!"

But my mom was calling me from the house, "Polly, you must . . . Polly, you must . . ."

Then I didn't know where I was, because my eyes were open and I was back in my room, and my mom was calling, "Polly, you must get up."

I felt great. The sun was shining in the windows and I was giggling to myself about the moving van.

I dressed, except for rebraiding my hair; my mom always did that. So I looked a little fuzzy headed when I landed in the kitchen.

Sis Hawkins sat at our kitchen table, her mouth full of my mom's toast.

"Susprich!" she said.

I must have looked like I'd been hit in the stomach because my mom led me gently to my chair.

"Look who came to see you," she said.

"Polly told me all about hiking and all," Sis said quickly, "so I decided I'd come over and walk her to school, her being such a good hiker and all. Ha. Ha. Ha."

My mother smiled and I tried to laugh.

"Anyway," Sis continued, "I would have waited outside, but I saw you, Mrs. Banks, cooking up a storm so I knocked on the door, and you said, 'Want some toast?' and I said, 'Yes ma'am.' It sure is good toast. I thought it sure would be a surprise for Polly. Didn't I surprise you? Huh!"

She poked me in the ribs with her fork and I nodded yes.

"Then, your mom said, 'Have an egg!' which I am. You sure do cook good eggs, Mrs. Banks."

I couldn't tell whether my mom was charmed or alarmed.

She spoke slowly. "Why thank you . . . ?"

"Sis Hawkins," Sis said. "My name is Sis Hawkins."

Silence.

My mom stirred her coffee, and I tried to swallow anything.

Silence.

Sis sat up inspired. "What do you cook your eggs in, Mrs. Banks?"

My mom talked a full minute on butter versus bacon drippings.

It was time to go when Sis said, "It certainly was fun talking to you about cooking."

"My pleasure, Sis," my mom said with a relaxed grin.

She was still grinning when she stood at the door watching us leave.

I was halfway down the drive when I realized I was going to school fuzzy headed with messy braids, and my mom hadn't noticed.

We walked a block silently. I was just busting with questions — what was she doing trying so hard to make a good impression? did she really care that much for eggs? what was going on?

She must have read my thoughts, because she said, "I didn't stay last night because I didn't feel like staying, and I came over this morning because I felt like coming over. Understand?"

"You always do what you like!" I said.

"Don't you!"

"No. Y...Y...Y...Y...Yes. I m...m...m...m...mean..."

Sis interrupted. "Tell me again about us, I mean you, sleeping out and all."

I gave it to her again about my outdoor experiences. I threw in something about cooking over a campfire, mentioning eggs especially since she seemed to have such a case on them.

She stopped before the school grounds. "And you're never scared to sleep outside?"

"Nothing to be scared of," I said.

"Not even wild animals?"

I started to say no. But I remembered the elk, then I thought of Dr. Maxie and my freakdom. My stuttering came back like a bad case of pimples. "S...S...S...Sometimes. I m...m...m...m...mean you have to b...b...b... be careful."

Sis stepped back as if my stuttering was a shock.

The bell rang and we had to run to be on time. I was almost glad to be wrapped in Dixieland for another day. At least I didn't have to think about elks and shrinks.

After school, Sis showed me the shady bank where everybody in the neighborhood played. It was tucked away on a wooded un-buildable lot. The kids had made a slide in the dirt. Sis said it was clay. There were trees to climb and a small creek.

The afternoon was great. The January sun was so warm we had to take off our coats.

We were pretty grungy looking from climbing and sliding when my dad came home from his trip.

(My dad, unlike my mom, doesn't care about cleanliness. You should see the bath-room after he shaves. Messy!)

He jumped from the car and tossed me

high in the air. He's strong, even if he sits at a desk all day handling plastic.

"How's my babe?" he yelled.

"F...F...Fine," I said, wiggling free. I ran and pulled Sis forward. "I want you to m... m...m...meet..." I began.

"Sis Hawkins," she said. "I'm Polly's new friend." She held out her hand.

One nice thing about my dad, he's a warm welcomer. He gave Sis's hand a real jiggle, talking all the time. "Any friend of Polly's is a friend of mine."

I watched Sis give my dad the once over.

"Hey," he said. "Why don't you wait until I say hello to Polly's mom and I get off my tie. We'll shoot a few baskets."

"Great!" Sis said.

It was getting dark when Sis left. I walked her to the mailbox.

She paused. "You have swell parents."

"What's wrong with having swell p...p... p...p...parents?"

"Nothing," she said, heading home.

Freaky. What was she getting at?

I watched her shuffling along. She shook her head as if she were arguing with herself.

My mom called me to supper. I was hungry ... as an elk.

Spelldown

Friday morning Sis was at the breakfast
table talking to my mom.

My mom had made waffles, and usually she
only makes waffles on Sundays.

"Terrific!" Sis said.

Walk to school, ditto.

Trouble began at the end of the school day.

Instead of history, we were having a spelldown. Two sides lined up. I was on the Governors' wall, Sis was with the Confederacy.

I was eliminated immediately.

"*Fantasy*," Miss Patterson said to me.

"Fantasy," I said. "P..."

"Down."

Some words were easy like *private* and

dipper. Others were toughies like *persimmon* or *orangutan*.

Miss Patterson was having a fine time throwing words at scared kids. Who likes to be hit with *persimmon?*

At the end of four rounds, two still stood — Sis and Cynthia.

Cynthia had just spelled *persevere*.

Miss Patterson said, *"Paragon*, Sis."

Sis shrugged her shoulders like who-cares-what-it-means. "Paragon," she said. "P...A...R...A, para. G...O...N, gon. Paragon." Sis grinned at her team and shook her hands over her head like a boxer.

I could see Miss Patterson disapproved of champions.

"That will be enough, Sis," she said.

With the next round of words, Cynthia spelled *warrior* carefully. Sis spelled *calcify* so confidently she did it sing-song.

"I said, that's enough," Miss Patterson said harshly. When she turned to give Cynthia her word, Sis stuck out her tongue.

May and I giggled.

Miss Patterson whirled. "Stop that!"

We were quiet, but Miss Patterson kept eying Sis suspiciously.

The words kept coming. Cynthia's seemed

to be getting easier while Sis's got more difficult — *heinous* and *putrefaction*, for example.

Sis was riding high. She kept making faces and clowning. Of course our team was having a fine time.

The more fun we had, the stranger Miss Patterson acted. She got dreamier and dreamier. After Sis spelled *justification*, Miss Patterson paused for such a long time, I was uncomfortable. She stood looking out the window like we weren't even there.

Cynthia broke the spell. "Miss Patterson," she said, "what's my next word?"

Miss Patterson shook herself like she was waking up. She paid no attention to Cynthia but marched straight to her big private dictionary and began turning pages furiously. Finally, she slammed the book closed and said, *"Trousseau,* Sis. You can't get that one."

It had happened so fast no one thought to yell, "Unfair!" "It's Cynthia's word!" "Foreign words aren't legal!"

I leaned forward, expecting something — I didn't know what.

Sis squinched up her face and wet her lips. "Trousseau," she said slowly. "T...R..." She

48

stopped and looked at the ceiling, thinking. "U..." she said.

"Down!" Miss Patterson shouted. It's T... R...O. It's T...R...O...U...S...S...E...A...U." She began jumping up and down like a little kid. "You missed. You missed."

Miss Patterson smiled in Cynthia's direction. I guess Sis didn't think she'd be caught. "Crazy," she said, too clearly. "C...R...A...Z... Y." Then she crossed her eyes and went back to her desk in a weird knees-in toes-in walk.

The class fell apart. We giggled, then we laughed. Nobody would stop when Sis tried to hush us.

Boom!

"Stop it! Stop it!" Miss Patterson screamed. She thought we were laughing at her.

The class's laughter shriveled. I was scared. I looked at Sis; that was a mistake.

Miss Patterson blew. "Sis Hawkins, it's all your fault. No one can laugh at me. I must have respect. I must have order. No one can laugh at me. No one . . ." On and on she went, making no sense at all.

Finally, she slumped into her chair and gazed off unhappily.

When the bell rang, we all fled for the door.

I thought Sis would wait up for me, but she was running away fast.

"See you tomorrow," she yelled in a funny voice like she was crying.

I tried to follow, but she was too quick.

"Sis wouldn't be crying," I said to myself. "No, Sis Hawkins wouldn't cry."

I walked home alone trying to put some distance between me and Miss Patterson.

I'll give you some advice right now — NEVER LAUGH AT A TYRANT!

Signs

I was on my bike by 9:00 on Saturday, heading for Sis's.

"I have to warn you my mother expresses her personality," she said, when she invited me over.

The house looked like all the others in Happy Valley, something my mother would call, "Enchanting!" It was surrounded by a bright wintergreen lawn. Shrubs were clipped, and the white paint looked fresh.

Sis told me that her mother had a gardener named Otto Frink who lived in the basement with his wife, Belle. Otto had been a counterfeiter who made over a million dollars, got caught, and served in a Federal penitentiary.

He's a gardener now, because with his record, he couldn't find any work.

Low soft music, Indian stuff, caught me outside the door. I had to knock three times to be heard. Sis came out and put her finger to her lips to hush me. I could see she was just as perky as always. I walked in. The house was dark and smelled of fall roses.

I peered through the archway into the living room.

There were five women in black tights standing on their heads.

I staggered backward, and stepped on something soft—Oliver Wendell Holmes, the poodle.

The dog yelped.

I screamed.

Sis yelled.

Five pairs of legs hit the floor at once.

I started for the door.

Sis nabbed me. The music had stopped. I saw through my confusion that the ladies right-side-up looked like my mother would if she had had on black tights and had just come off her head.

Sis pushed me before the one in the center. It was her mother, because there was the same black snaky hair and round face grown up.

"Claudia," Sis said. "I want you to meet my friend, Polly Banks. You know . . ."

"The one that . . ."

"Yep."

I guess I hesitated, but Claudia or Sis's mother or Ms. Hawkins (I'm never quite sure what to call her) gave me a big hug and said, "Shalom!" which means *peace* in Hebrew.

She added in English, "Scoot!"

"Let's have something to eat," Sis said. "I'm starving."

The music twanged and the feet rose in the air. I knew things were back to normal, whatever that meant in the Hawkins house. Even Oliver Wendell Holmes had resumed his nap by the archway.

I took off my jacket and put it on the pile of coats by the stairs; then I eased inside the kitchen.

Unlike my mother's — which had everything including the salt and pepper behind closed doors — this kitchen had everything out. Not one single inch of space was vacant. The plants alone could furnish a florist shop. Jars of stuff were everywhere — beads, noodles sitting among dried flowers, dried herbs, old Christmas decorations, hollow Easter eggs, and macrame hangings, precious objects.

But the most remarkable thing was the signs. As I returned to the house more and more, I memorized the one printed on the refrigerator.

The sign said, "Order means light and peace, inward liberty and free command over oneself."

I wished Miss Patterson would memorize it.

More signs were over doors, above windows, on mirrors, lettered on coffee cups, all different.

After a big bowl of granola and bananas, Sis showed me everywhere, from the basement — no boxes marked BOXES down there — to the attic.

In the basement she introduced me to Mr. Frink, who was sitting outside the small apartment that had been made out of a recreation room. He was drawing a picture of George Washington, "Just for fun," he said.

Ms. Frink was upstairs on her head.

Second floor, her mother's room decorated with funny furniture, more flowers and signs. "We shall overcome — Martin Luther King" was over the doorway.

Sis's room, more of the same.

We passed a study piled high with heavy books.

"My dad's stuff," Sis said. She cocked her head then and paused. I had never seen such a change. She talked so low I had trouble hearing her. "My dad died two years ago. He was a doctor. I miss him, but Claudia says you remember by actions." Then she eyed me as if I was going to say something silly. "That's settled."

I said, "Okay."

Sis began talking a mile a minute. "We used to live in the city. Claudia said it was getting too polluted and the suburbs were getting too stuck-up, so she decided the suburbs needed yoga and us. That's why I'm in Mandalay. I'm supposed to think of myself as a missionary, you know?"

I nodded and smiled, suddenly feeling a little missionary-ish myself.

"We moved here in September. Claudia's going to law school as soon as we get settled. Excuse the mess," she said.

We were moving toward the stairs, circling a precarious arrangement of boxes and old magazines.

Sis stopped. "Claudia's going to be a judge, and I'm going to be a doctor like my father. What are you going to be?"

We were standing at the head of the steps. The January sun was streaming through the dusty windows onto the dark patterned oriental rugs. Smells of dried herbs and roses, burned bacon and coffee grounds mixed deliciously with faint smells of fish fertilizer.

"I'm going to be a si...si...si...si...si..."

Sis's mother yelled, "Someone let Oliver out!"

Sis leaped down the steps and opened the front door.

I was amazed. I was about to say I wanted to be a psychiatrist like Dr. Maxie, and I hadn't thought of her since our first visit last Wednesday. Something really weird had happened to me in that office.

Then I thought, something really weird happens in this house.

Ms. Hawkins

After Sis let Oliver out and in, Ms. Hawkins waved to us, inviting us to join the group. The exercises were over and the women were sitting, sewing, knitting and talking.

Sis whispered, "This is my mom's Saturday morning liberated women's-yoga-sewing-circle-discussion-group."

"I see," I said, a little confused.

We perched beside Ms. Hawkins and listened.

Otto's wife, Belle, was telling about prisons. When she said the warden was "for obeying rules regardless of people's feelings," I noticed Ms. Hawkins put her arm around Sis.

Then Belle spoke about Otto's guard, Jones. "Crazy cruel," she said.

"Tell them what he did," Ms. Hawkins said.

Belle spoke quickly. "Otto said Jones picked on the weaknesses of the prisoners. One lisped, another was crippled. Jones mocked them before the whole cellblock as if they could help themselves. The other prisoners ached for their friends, but what could they do?"

"But prisoners are supposed to be punished," one lady by the archway interrupted.

"They're human still," Belle replied.

The lady ducked her head. "Of course."

Belle continued. "Eventually Jones made everyone suffer. He began to hold back their mail, the only treasured touch with home. Otto said he saw grown men beg and weep for a letter."

"That's terrible," someone said, I couldn't see who.

Belle's voice grew so low I had to lean forward to hear.

"I think Otto was right when he said Jones had to prove his superiority by hurting others." She paused. "I tried to do something. I wrote the warden, the Governor, the President. I got back three form letters." She shrugged her shoulders. "Life was unbearable, so they struck."

"Attica!"

"Not with clubs," Belle said. "They just stopped eating until they were heard."

I listened as Ms. Hawkins said to Sis, "Gandhi."

I turned back to Belle as she was saying, "They drove the guard crazier." She laughed lightly. "It was strange. He roared around the cellblock yelling about disobedience, threatening, showing how sick he really was. Of course, he was fired, though Otto said he saw him last week in a uniform. I guess he's found somebody else to terrorize."

The room was quiet, then there was a lot of talk.

I watched Belle. She was the first convict's wife I had ever seen close up, and she looked just like one of my mother's League of Women Voters friends.

The meeting was over when the hall clock chimed 12:00.

The talk in the living room changed to "It's late . . ." "I have to run."

Ms. Hawkins' voice was firm. "We'll take up next week where we left off."

The women moved quickly to gather their coats. The hall was empty except for Sis, me, and Ms. Hawkins. I reached for my jacket and put my arm in my sleeve.

Ms. Hawkins nabbed me. "Where are you going?" she said, zipping off my jacket and throwing it on the bannister, heading me into the kitchen.

All the serious talk was over. She stood with her hands on her hips. "Tell me all about yourself."

The switch in my throat went into stutter. "M...M...M..." I stammered.

Sis was no help; no finger up the nose or anything. Then I looked at Ms. Hawkins and she had the same expression I recognized as a Maxie look. "What would you like to know?" I said.

"Where did you get that yellow hair? When did you move here? Sis, what did you do with the butter? This place is a mess. Let's see, Polly, tell me what's your favorite dish? Sis, where is the butter? Sis, you cook. I want to talk to Polly. Somebody let Oliver out." She paused to give me one of the Hawkins nail-em looks, but her voice was kind. "I really want to know."

"My mother. January 2. Anything," I said.

"That's better." She sat solidly at the table while Sis fixed Hawkins' Hash. (Two cans of potatoes, one can of corned beef, salt, pepper and pray.)

I chatted about Seattle and climbing mountains. When I got to hiking halfway up Mt. Rainier, Ms. Hawkins said, "That must be why you're such as good kicker."

I was pleased she had even heard about my kicking. "I guess," I said.

I started telling about the forests and the wilderness; she nodded like she understood everything.

"You sure do love that country."

"Yes," I said, then I thought I'd add a little thing my mom always said, "It's the only one we've got."

Sis served up the hash.

We took our plates into the living room, and Sis started a fire in the fireplace. It was cozy. Finally, Ms. Hawkins yawned and said, "I think I'll go upstairs and read."

"Nap," Sis whispered.

The afternoon slipped away. Sis brought out her pastels, and we did some of that, then played Sorry. At 3:00, Sis said, "Let's take a walk."

The air was cool, brittle. The creek that

ran beside the school also bordered Sis's. The woods along its banks were dark and spooky, but we jumped from wet rock to wet rock, climbed over trunks of rotting trees and fell into dry leaves.

The sun was almost down when I returned home smelling like Hawkins, fall roses and fish fertilizer and creek, dry leaves and tree rot.

"What did you do today?" my mom said, hurrying to take off my coat.

"Did you have a nice time?" my dad said.

"F...F...F...F...Fine," I said, plopping in front of the TV. I wanted to keep the day to myself.

"Elizabeth," my dad said. "When are we going to have supper? I'm hungry. I bet Polly is too."

"G...G...G...Guess so," I said.

My mother went fluttery. "We're having chicken cooked exactly the way you like it, Polly, with mushrooms . . ." She was in the kitchen by then; her voice was fainter. "String beans with almonds, apple pie for dessert."

Suddenly I thought, my mother is not Claudia Hawkins, and I resented it.

The supper was served, and my mom and

dad carried on the usual conversation trying to get me to join in, but something was stopping me. I couldn't understand it. Part of me wished to punish them for not being what I wanted them to be; the other part felt ashamed for keeping all my news back.

It didn't help, them being so nice.

They let me watch TV long after 10:00 and my mom brought hot chocolate to my room. She sat on the bed and I almost started telling about Ms. Hawkins, Hawkins' Hash, and meeting my first convict's wife.

I leaned forward.

She leaned forward.

I guess we looked ridiculous.

I leaned back. She must have known it was no use, because she leaned back too.

She smiled that hurt smile.

I said, "Good night."

She kissed me on the cheek and said, "Oh, Polly."

Somehow I felt I had failed again.

Trouble With Explosives

My second appointment with Dr. Maxie came the next Wednesday.

Now, let me tell you about having a shrink even if the shrink is as cool as Dr. Maxie. *You don't want anyone to know.*

It's difficult on a friendship if you're trying to hide something.

That afternoon, Sis ran after me yelling, "Wait up!"

"I gotta go," I said over my shoulder.

She ran alongside singing, "If you gotta go, you gotta go . . ." She pulled me to a halt. "Where exactly are you going?" she said.

My face must have shown something closed off, because Sis stepped back like a snake had bitten her. "Go on, then," she said.

You guessed it; I stuttered something wild. "I c...c...can't t...t...t...tell you." It was a waste of breath. Sis was halfway to the corner.

I was in great shape for a shrink.

Dr. Maxie was waiting for me at the door. I plunked down in the chair, crossing my arms before me, madlike. I guess I was saying, "Try and make me talk."

Silence.

Dr. Maxie sat in the opposite chair. "You look like you've had it."

I exploded. "Y...Y...You're d...d...d...darn right." I told her how Sis was mad at me. "I d...d...d...don't want to b...b...be sitting in this d...d...dumb old office. I want to b...b...b...be p...p...playing b...b...b...basketb...b...b...ball with Sis Hawkins who is the b...b...b...best b...b...basketb...b...baller in the whole world."

I was beginning to feel a little foolish. "Nothing p...p...p...personal," I said.

Dr. Maxie smiled. "Tell me about Sis."

By the time I finished about Sis talking eggs with my mom, and about the Hawkins' funny house, I must have gone on nonstop for fifteen minutes. When I came to Miss Patterson putting Sis down, I could see Dr. Maxie was touched. She shook her head like something was hurting her.

"What about this Miss Patt . . ." she began.

But a weird thing happened, I interrupted. "And I didn't tell my mom anything . . . at all."

I expected Dr. Maxie to say, "Shame on you." Instead, she said, "You wanted to keep it to yourself."

I nodded, but for some reason tears rose in my eyes.

"You really admire Sis."

I nodded again.

"You didn't tell her about me."

I shook my head.

"People who love you want to know," she said kindly.

"N...N...N...No!" I shouted, feeling very guilty all at once. I looked at the ceiling trying to think of something to change the subject, then I sat up straight. "Why do I stutter?"

"Only you can tell why you stutter," she said.

"B...B...B...But, sometimes I'm all right."

Dr. Maxie leaned back, relaxed. "Part of your problem is you have trouble with explosives."

"TNT?"

"It can be that dangerous."

"What are they?"

"Some letters like Bs and Ps are called explosives. You have to push them out of your mouth. They are hard for you, but you will control them . . . if . . ."

"Bs and Ps," I said. Then the weird thing happened again. "P...P...P...Polly B...B...B... Banks." I said. "I have trouble with myself."

"Maybe you just have trouble talking about yourself—Polly Banks," Dr. Maxie said.

My head was too full; I was silent for the rest of the hour.

At the door, Dr. Maxie said, "See you next week."

I could tell from her eyes I was doing okay.

I skipped down the hall and jumped into my mom's car. "Dr. Maxie told me I have trouble with expl...pl...pl...plosives," I began and continued explaining as we drove off.

When I finished, she said, "Who needs fire-crackers on the Fourth when we have you!"

We felt so good we had to stop for an ice cream cone.

"Pistaschio, please," I said.

Bad Business

Dinner was different that night. Don't misunderstand me. I still stuttered; it just wasn't such a big deal anymore. I didn't feel like I was being interviewed by my parents.

I told my dad about my trouble with explosives, and he said, "Isn't that interesting."

Not, "Go on!" or "Tell me more."

And my mom didn't lean forward when she brought me my hot chocolate to bed. Unfortunately, as she lingered at the door, she saw my room too clearly.

"This is terrible," she said. "Look at those clothes on the floor."

"I've been b...b...b...busy," I said.

"I've been busy too," she said, stooping to pick up my dress.

I started to get out of bed to stop her before she stooped too far and discovered where I stored old socks, comic books and dirty dishes.

"Look what's under this bed!" she said.

"Sorry," I mumbled.

"Young lady, you'll straighten this room out tomorrow."

"B...B...B...But I want to p...p...p...play ball."

"You'll come right home from school," she said.

"Rats," I said.

But the next day I woke wanting to jump up and get going. The good feeling even continued through cleaning my room.

The week zipped by. I was in high gear.

"Cool it," Sis said.

"B...B...B...But things are great!" I said.

"I don't feel so great," she began, but she changed the subject. "Let's play tag."

Ever since the spelldown Miss Patterson had been after her, pestering her. Sis hadn't turned in the right assignment. Sis had to miss the field trip to the Capitol because she talked too much. Sis had to sit outside the room for two hours, because she had run in the halls.

The next Wednesday, things boiled up again.

We had returned from recess; Miss Patterson was seeing about something in the office. A couple of kids were playing tic-tac-toe on the blackboard until Sis began drawing Snoopy shooting baskets.

It was funny, because the face on the basketball was as sour as Miss Patterson.

When she appeared at the door, Sis had to erase fast. Of course the kids laughed.

"Stop it!" Miss Patterson screamed, just like the last time she thought we were laughing at her.

Sis took her seat, but Miss Patterson was still upset, and she stayed that way all afternoon.

When May made a mistake in Language Arts, Miss Patterson blew. "If you weren't so fat, you'd remember!" she said.

May was crying when she mumbled, "I'm sorry."

Bad business.

Wednesday was shrink day. The bad business was still on my mind. I decided to talk to Dr. Maxie about Miss Patterson. But, when I arrived in the office, Dr. Maxie had on her coat and said, "How about some outdoor conversation?"

We left by the back door and walked slowly in the quiet woods that surrounded the building. All those trees made me chat about mountains, not Miss Patterson.

I was saying, "It's funny about climbing too. You think you only have one more hill before the top. Then you get to the top of that hill, and there's still more . . . and more . . ." when Dr. Maxie interrupted.

"That's like stuttering," she said.

"How's that?"

"You're on one hill now, but . . ."

"I'm not cured," I said.

Dr. Maxie smiled. "Just remember you'll have other hills. Don't be discouraged." She looked at her watch. "It's getting late."

"But I wanted to talk about my teacher . . ."

"Miss Patterson."

She was waiting for me to go on, but I knew it wouldn't be fair. I needed a whole hour for her. At least. "Next week," I said.

Tyrants

What is a tyrant?
Choose one.
1. Something on a railroad line. "A train runs on wood tyrants."
2. A scarf usually two feet long and worn by a tall man.
3. A person who rules by fear.

If you chose number three, you are correct. If you say, "For example, Miss Lenora Patterson," you are double right.

I'm a little ahead of myself. The last of January brought a cold front. I put on two sweaters, a coat, a muffler and gloves, but I still had to jump up and down to keep warm waiting for school to start. On Monday it was so freezing the class voted to stay inside even if they had to be with Miss Patterson.

That was cold.

The idea seemed harmless—friends getting together in the room under Miss Patterson's gaze.

When the recess bell rang, Sis came to my desk and we played Hangman, talking and giggling about the shows on TV. (I'd better tell you now that Sis and I watched the same shows before we met. How about that!)

We eventually attracted a group—May, Sarah and Cynthia.

I don't know what made me look at Miss Patterson, but she was watching me so closely, she gave me the willys.

I poked Sis.

"Your turn," Sis said. She didn't catch Miss Patterson's funny look.

On Tuesday the cold front passed. Although it was still below freezing, the winter sun was out and it was bearable. Sis pulled me down the steps heading for the icy mud and the frozen creek. As I started down, I paused. The hair on my neck rose up. I knew Miss Patterson was watching us from the window.

There was something about her standing there that reminded me of the elk again. I was scared.

"D...D...D...Do you s...s...s...s...see Miss P...P...P...P...Patterson?"

I was stuttering so hard Sis grew impatient. "Let's run," she said. "It's too cold."

My hair was still riding up my neck as we walked home later. "Why does Miss P...P...P..."

"Patterson," Sis helped.

". . . hate p...p...p...p...people to have f...f...f..."

"Fun," Sis finished.

"She's so mean and all."

Sis stopped. I could tell she was about to say something silly.

"Seriously," I said.

She shivered, like a rabbit was running over her grave. "She's a tyrant," she said. "A person who hates freedom. But I'm not scared of her."

That night I went to sleep carefree. I didn't know I was on one hill looking at another and another.

Wednesday started peacefully. The flag group had passed; the flags were replaced in their stands. The class was restless.

I was daydreaming out the window. Miss Patterson usually had a quiet meditation between the patriotic scene and the Pledge, but this day she called my name immediately. "Polly Banks."

I overturned my chair jumping up. The class twittered.

"Yes ma'am," I said.

"Lead us in the Pledge," she said.

As the class got to their feet and faced the flag, I moved away from my desk and put my hand over my heart.

I opened my mouth confidently.

"I p...p...p...p...pledge allegiance to the F...F...F...F...F..."

The class was ahead of me, behind me. There were giggles, snickers. I looked at Miss Patterson for help; she looked only at the flag.

Everything returned in that moment, the elk, the fear of freakdom, all the humiliation and embarrassment I thought I had forgotten.

I was alone.

"F...F...F...F...F...Flag of the United States of Amer...mer...mer...mer...mer...mer...mer...merica."

The class copied my stutter, laughing, stammering.

"America. One Nation under God, in...in...in...in...in..." I felt the wetness on my cheeks before I knew I was crying. Miss Patterson blurred as I concentrated. It had to be over soon.

"Stop it!" someone yelled. It was Sis standing before the flags with her arms raised.

No one paid any attention.

"Stop it!" she screamed again and waved her arms as if they were magic wands; she caught the Confederate flag and the Georgia flag.

"Grab them," someone yelled.

They fell with a flop on the floor.

"Oh, no!"

"Sis is going to get it."

"Stop it!" Sis yelled for the third time.

The class hushed.

I watched Miss Patterson. She staggered backward as if she were ill, staring at the toppled flags.

The class was as still as in the movies, before the firing squad says "Fire!"

"You desecrated the flags," she roared.

"They were laughing at Polly," Sis screamed back.

"Go to your seats."

We all slithered to our chairs. I wiped my eyes with the backs of my hands. Then I looked quickly around the room. Sis was smiling at me. She was the only one. Everyone else was tense, waiting for the usual Patterson fit.

Instead, Miss Patterson was like ice, standing at her desk with her hands on the back of her chair. I saw her fingers were clutching the wood so tightly her knuckles were white. She was smiling a smile I would like to forget but can't.

"Well, Sis Hawkins," she said slowly. "You are to write the Pledge of Allegiance five hundred times."

Sis was grinning like you do when you get kicked in the shins. You feel the pain gradually. "Five hundred times?" Sis repeated. She cocked her head as if to push the thought through her mind. "That's not fair," she said.

Miss Patterson was looking at Sis like Sis hadn't said anything.

"They were laughing at Polly." Sis's voice got soft.

Miss Patterson had her. "Six hundred times."

"I can't do it," Sis said, looking at me.

"Seven hundred times."

I jumped up. "Miss Patterson, may I go to the bathroom?"

Whatever I did, worked. When I returned, the class was bent over their books. Sis wasn't. She had her pad out and was writing hard.

I didn't think twice; I got out my pad too. *I pledge allegiance to the Flag,* I started. When the bell rang, I had only written four and my fingers felt like they were a hundred years old.

Sis wrote through recess, sitting on the school steps. It was still cold. She had to stop every line to blow on her icy fingers. I plopped beside her, shivering, and angry for forgetting to bring my Pledges along.

"Rats. Rats. Rats," Sis said.

"How many?" I asked.

"Six."

"I did four in the room," I said. "Only six hundred and ninety to go."

I knew I had made a mistake. Sis tossed her head proudly. Her cheeks were red; I could see she was furious.

"You can't help me," she said, getting up.

I followed her into the school. "How are you going to do it alone?"

"I'll do it. I'll do it. That . . . That . . ." she sputtered. "Miss Patterson. I'll show her."

I had to run to catch up. She dashed for the room.

"You'll d...d...d...d...do it," I said.

And I tried, honestly tried, to feel like Sis would do it, and everything would be fine. But, by lunch time, my stomach was as tight as a rubberband about to go b-wango. The switch in my throat kept over on stutter.

I couldn't eat. Sis grabbed bites between ends of lines. Her writing was nonstop. During lunch I saw tables of boys and girls squint at Sis sympathetically as if she had been paddled by the principal, been demoted — she was a celebrity.

"How many?" I asked as we dumped our trays on the clean-up shelf.

She only shook her head.

By 2:30 I was in such bad shape, tears kept rising in my eyes. My stomach hurt and I wanted to get away from everyone — Miss Patterson, May, Cynthia, even Sis.

I seemed to get better when the last bell rang; the cold air in my face helped.

Sis joined me silently. At the corner where we usually decide whose house is going to be "it," Sis said, "I gotta go home."

"Me too," I said.

Sis was under a prison sentence, I had caused it, and we had a crazy warden.

I knew how Otto Frink must have felt.

Breakthrough

My mom let me in. She was full of business.

"We've got to hurry. There's Dr. Maxie, and I want to drop something off at the cleaners. Then, I'll pick up some groceries . . ." I guess she must have noticed me following her around, because she said, "Are you all right?"

I guess it was her cool hand on my hot head or something, because I cried and talked, cried and talked.

"Miss Patterson made Sis write the Pledge seven hundred times and it's all my fault . . . and I can't help . . . Sis can't do it . . . I hate that school and that teacher . . . Miss Patterson is a warden and we're in prison . . . and

80

we can't do anything . . . I hate moving . . . I hate stuttering and I want a friend like Sis . . . And she's in trouble because of me . . ."

She led me to the sofa and sat beside me as I cried. Things were all mixed up. I'd tell her about my standing before the class, then I'd tell her about hating to move. I'd tell her about the seven hundred Pledges, then I'd tell her about me feeling so lonely.

She put her arms around me and held me when I cried, let me sit up and talk when I wanted to.

"There. There. There," she said, not fluttery or organized. "I know . . . I know."

My hiccups started. She had gotten a wet rag for my eyes when the phone rang.

My mom said, "Dr. Maxie!" and I felt more miserable. I had missed the appointment.

"Polly's had a problem at school," she told her. "She's crying and terribly upset . . . Yes, I know . . . Of course we will. My husband and I . . . I'll tell her. Thank you for calling. Yes, we will. You can be sure, next week."

She returned to the sofa, smiling like Dr. Maxie. "She was concerned," she said.

"I stood her up," I wailed.

"She told me to tell you, 'Remember the little hills.' "

My mom stayed right there. I finally dozed off. As the afternoon faded, I would wake up and see her sitting quietly in the satin chair.

Later I half-heard my mom talking to my dad in the entry hall. Her voice was low. "Miss Patterson . . . the Pledge . . . Sis and Polly . . . seven hundred times."

I sat up quick when my dad yelled, "That no-count woman! Who does she think she is!"

"Hush, Polly's asleep."

"I'm going to call her," he said.

His heavy footsteps echoed across the hall, then I heard pages of the telephone book flipping. All the time my mother was saying, "Should we? Do you think . . ."

My father cursed. "She can't get away with this. What's her name. P . . . Palson, Paton, Patterson."

"Lenora Patterson . . . but Dr. Maxie said . . ."

"Here it is."

I heard dialing.

"No," I screamed, running to the phone and jerking the receiver out of his hand. "You can't!"

You should have seen their faces. Stunned.

The receiver clicked down; the telephone book fell to the floor.

Suddenly Miss Patterson's face floated before me; she had on her triumphant smile. "I won't let you," I said.

My dad squinched up his mouth like he was thinking hard. My mom was shaking her head like she was trying to tell him something without using words.

"Okay, Toots," he said. "If that's the way you want it."

My ears were playing tricks on me. I turned to my mom to test her. "You mean it?"

"Absolutely," she said, heading for the kitchen.

My dad was waiting for an explanation, I guess, because he was leaning against the wall patiently.

"You see," I began, not sure where I was going. "I kinda feel it's my business, I mean . . . It's my school, you know." He nodded. "It's between Sis and me and that dumb old teacher, you know?"

"Un huh," he said.

"I just don't want you to call."

"You can handle it," he said.

I nodded.

He shook my hand like a businessman. "Never doubted it for a moment."

My dad sat in his chair and began unfolding the evening paper. I felt a little foolish.

I perched on the arm of the chair. "Miss Patterson is a tyrant," I said.

He turned the page. "Probably," he said. Then he put the paper down. "You know, there are many people in the world who can't help but let their unhappiness spread over others," he said. He must have seen my worried look. "But, her unhappiness won't rub off on you."

"Not Sis either?"

"Certainly not Sis." My dad winked at me.

Later that night I think I heard my mom laughing, although I was pretty tired. She was saying, "Polly didn't stutter. She's getting better."

Sis looked terrible the next morning. Her eyes were ringed with black circles, and she didn't even wave when she saw me. Her hand hung down like it was broken.

"Six hundred and seventy to go," she said.

We walked silently.

"Did you tell your mother?" I asked. Sis looked ahead. "I told my mom and dad about everything . . ."

"What did they do?" Sis interrupted.

84

"My dad started to call her up and bless her out . . ." Sis gave me one of her I'm-disappointed looks. "But, I said he couldn't."

"Me too . . ."

"Your mom wanted . . ."

"To call."

"What did you say?"

"I said if she gave the old nut any satisfaction, I'd grow up to be a conservative."

I didn't laugh. I have a conservative relative — undrunk Uncle Harry.

Sis continued. "My mom said she was going to stand on her head all day and think about it, but I think she's going to call your mom."

"My mom!" I stopped walking.

Sis had to call me to get me going. "Hurry up. I've got two Pledges to do before school starts."

"W...W...W...Wait up," I stammered.

All that day I worried about my mom and Ms. Hawkins talking on the phone. Would my mom hear all that Indian music in the background? Would Ms. Hawkins hear the hum of our vacuum cleaner? What if they got together?

The scene floated before me. Ms. Hawkins

would come into our house, take one look, and say, "No child of mine is staying in such a clean place!"

Then, my mother would grab me and say, "Get your Sis away from our tidy child!"

Sis and I would be dragged apart, weeping.

Dr. Maxie said I had a rich fantasy life.

Quotation Time

The day passed. Ten Pledges later for Sis, six hundred and sixty to go, we were walking home. At the decision corner we spoke at once. "I'd better go home," we said and didn't laugh.

My mom was out. A note rested among the milk and cookies. *Business,* it said. *Be back at five. Love, Mom.*

I sat around watching cartoons, and I hate cartoons, but they are better than thinking.

My mom returned at dark, hugging me so efficiently I thought I smelled a League of Women Voters meeting on her. It never took long for her to get involved.

"How many?" she said.

"Six hundred and sixty," I said.

She grinned. "She's probably at six hundred and fifty. That Sis writes fast." Then she skipped, honestly skipped, into the kitchen, humming. She must have said something bright at the meeting.

I followed her and sat on the stool while she cooked. She told me how she had to write "I will never sit on Billy Boy Handson's lap in the lunchroom" two hundred times when she was my age. Pretty soon we were laughing.

I told her about May Biggs and her chocolate cake, Sarah Coots and her funny ways, Rob Peters and how out of place he looks being so young. "They are freaks," I said, stopping before I said, *like me*.

Then she did a funny thing; she took a deep breath like what she was going to say was difficult to get out.

I leaned forward.

"That reminds me of when I was in school and felt sort of freakish . . ." she began.

"You!"

"I was too tall," she said.

By the time she was through telling how hard it was for her waiting for everyone to catch up, how foolish she felt looking more like a teacher than a student, I felt better.

When my dad came in, he asked the same question, "How many?"

"Probably at six hundred and forty," I said. "That Sis writes fast."

"You better believe it."

But as we were eating dinner, my mother said, "Sis's mom called and said she'd like to come over and talk. I said 7:30 would be fine."

All the good feelings went swoosh out the window.

I know now I wanted to keep the Hawkinses to myself.

When the doorbell rang, things fuzzed over. I saw Ms. Hawkins standing there. Her afghan fur coat was open to reveal a long dress that had mirrors sewed all over. Her black hair was held back by a pink scarf with green rabbits running around the hem. It looked good on her I will admit.

I caught a glimpse of my mother's face. She was shocked.

My dad helped Ms. Hawkins in. My mother took her coat. Sis came bounding over to me and slapped me on the back. I could tell she was nervous.

The hall was filled with talk.

"How are you?"

"Glad to know you . . ."

"Call me Claudia . . ."

"Elizabeth, and this is Fred . . ."

"Do you like Atlanta?"

Regular things regular people say.

Then everyone moved into our sparkling clean living room. I sat on the footstool beside Sis. Ms. Hawkins plopped down on the satin chair, my mother's favorite, looking as surprising as a fever blister on your nose.

My mom served the coffee. My dad pulled up his leatherette recliner and was leaning over like he was in some business meeting.

No one spoke until my mom picked up her coffee cup and said, "Well, where shall we begin?"

Silence.

My mom and dad were looking at me like I should talk; Sis was looking at her mother like she should say something; Ms. Hawkins was looking at the ceiling like she wished she were standing on her head.

My dad broke the spell. "Before we get into the Pledges, I would like to hear what's been going on in school. How this started."

"T...T...T...Tell him about the spelldown," I said.

Sis started talking fast. "We had this spelling contest a week ago . . ."

"T...Ten days, maybe," I said.

"And Miss Patterson was throwing words around. I was the last one up . . ."

"Cynthia was the other one," I interrupted. "Sis got the hardest. *Trousseau!* Can you believe it!"

"It was *heinous* that made her mad . . . remember?" Sis said.

"And you spelled crazy and she thought . . ."

"I don't understand any of this," my dad said.

Ms. Hawkins said, "There was a spelling contest and Sis was one of the last standing. Miss Patterson kept giving her harder and harder words to make her lose."

"Unfair," Sis said.

"Miss Patterson had a fit that scared everybody," I said.

"Scared!" my dad said. "A teacher shouldn't make kids scared."

"She makes kids cry," Sis said.

"She picks on freaks too."

"She's a tyrant," Sis said.

"Like Hitler."

"She sure hates people to be free," Sis said.

My dad sat back, thinking. "So, that's why she picked on you, Sis."

Ms. Hawkins spoke clearly, "And that's why I haven't stepped in before. I think it's time Sis learned to deal with tyrants."

My mom said, "Oh, my!" like the idea was too strong for her. Then I watched her look at Ms. Hawkins like Ms. Hawkins wasn't dressed funny anymore. "I agree with Claudia," she said.

My dad was unconvinced. "I wanted to hear what Sis has to say since it really is between her and Miss Patterson."

Sis straightened up quickly. "I think I should show the old nut she can't get me."

"You agree, Polly?" my dad said.

I straightened up too. "Absolutely," I said.

"How about the Pledges?" my mom asked.

"I'm going to write every one of them."

The room got so quiet I thought nobody's breathing, then my mom looked at Ms. Hawkins. "There must be a better way," she said.

Ms. Hawkins' voice was low. "Sis isn't ready for that now — just saying she won't do them. One day she will." She smiled at Sis. "I'm sure of that."

"I think I understand," my mom said.

"You don't think we should tell Miss Heartbang?" my dad said.

"We could talk to Miss Patterson," my mom said.

"No!" we both shouted.

Then the meeting deteriorated. The parents began talking about "What if . . ." and "I think . . ." Then they started talking philosophy, "overviews . . ." and "I believes."

I knew everything was settled.

Suddenly I wasn't very happy; I had started it and Sis was doing all the work.

"I want to do something more," I said.

"You will."

We came back to the party when my mom said in her League of Women Voters voice, "Principles lie back of actions. America would be inconceivable without them."

Ms. Hawkins interrupted, "Woodrow Wilson."

After that it was like a tennis match. My mom would serve a quotation, and Ms. Hawkins would hit another one back. Sis, Dad and I had to sit and listen.

Ms. Hawkins said, "Jefferson said, 'I have sworn on the altar of God eternal hostility against every form of tyranny over the minds of men.' "

(That was on a sign in their upstairs bathroom.)

My mother smiled sweetly. "Of course my favorite Jefferson is 'All authority belongs to the people.'"

I began rooting for my mom.

"Yes, that's nice," Ms. Hawkins said, "but how about, 'We believe the only whole man is a free man.'"

"Franklin Roosevelt!"

Walls came tumbling down. The two began talking a mile a minute over what books they had read, what causes they had supported.

My mom talked about voter registration; Ms. Hawkins was on her prison reform trip.

I leaned back. I knew then I didn't have anything to worry about. Someone living in a TV-commercial-clean house can like someone living in a sign shop.

Getting It Done

When they left the hall was full of "I'll call you tomorrow . . ." from my mom, and "It's been wonderful getting to know you" from Ms. Hawkins.

The door shut and my dad said, "Those Hawkinses are something else!"

I hit the bed, bang, then I had this dream.

I was back in Seattle, and I was climbing this mountain with my mom and dad, Sis and her mother.

(Ms. Hawkins had on an orange Eskimo parka—weird!)

When we arrived at the Alpine Meadows, we stopped to catch our breath; the mountain was dead ahead. All of a sudden, the mountain sprouted an enormous American flag. The sky turned navy blue, and the stars shimmered in a circle. It could have been a poster saying, "America needs YOU!"

I heard distant thunder like a good war movie and music — "God Bless America."

We dropped our packs and stood at attention. When we said the Pledge, I didn't stutter.

Our voices grew so loud a small animal scurried from under a rock — a tiny elk. You guessed it, the elk's face was the face of Lenora Patterson.

As we got louder — I remember distinctly, we were on "One nation under God" — the elk took off down the mountain like she'd never stop. End of dream.

I woke up giggling, dressing quickly and ran down the stairs. I bounded into the kitchen. "Good morning," I said. "Isn't it a perfect day!"

My dad hugged me; my mom kissed my dad.

By Saturday, Sis stood at five hundred and fifty. Sis had written until her hand ached. No walks in the woods; nothing. Ms. Hawkins said she hadn't stood on her head for days and was feeling a little tense because Sis was not cooking.

The weekend passed. Monday she was at five hundred. I tried to help. I took her library books back and paid the 30¢ fine. I didn't even tell her. I served her hot chocolate and pulled her bedroom shade down on a beautiful day.

"Try for twenty-five a day," my mom suggested when Sis came over for a change of table and pencil.

On Tuesday night, my dad said he'd been caught in a sales meeting writing, "I pledge allegiance to the Osborn Plastic Company" He said the thing was intruding on his subconscious.

"That's not funny," my mom said, but my dad and I thought it was a great joke.

On Wednesday, I could hardly wait for school to be over so I could tell the news to Dr. Maxie.

Only when Miss Patterson said, "If you don't calm down, Polly, you'll have to stay in after school," did I settle.

It was funny how Miss Patterson had behaved since she sentenced Sis. If anything, she was less nervous and maybe a bit kinder, as if getting Sis out of the way was the only thing she needed to be happy.

The bell rang and I took off. I jumped up

and down waiting for my mom to get the car, and I was waiting for Dr. Maxie at her door when she opened it.

Her first words were, "You look like you're on top of the world."

Everything came out at once. "Sis is writing the Pledges. She's going to show that teacher. My mom likes Ms. Hawkins. My dad thinks they are something else. I'm talking all the time. S...S...S...Stuttering a little, b...b...b...but that doesn't matter. I told him not to call and he didn't . . ."

"Wait a minute," Dr. Maxie interrupted, "you'll have to go slower."

I took a deep breath and started again at the beginning. The spelldown, the Pledge, then Sis's punishment, me stopping my dad's calling, the meeting. When I said, "Miss Patterson is a tyrant," Dr. Maxie leaned forward.

"What does that mean to you?"

I paused. "It means she makes kids cry. She made me cry." I was having a hard time all of a sudden. "She scared us."

"She makes kids afraid of being themselves?" Dr. Maxie said.

"Yes," I said. "But Sis isn't scared. She's standing up to her," I added proudly.

98

"How about you?" Dr. Maxie said.

"I c...c...c...can't do anything!"

"You stood up to your dad about that telephone. You felt good about that."

"That's different."

"Is it?"

I was silent for a moment. "You mean it's the same thing!"

"You sometimes have to fight bravely for your rights . . . for your independence," Dr. Maxie said seriously.

"B...B...B...But, I can't," I stammered.

"It's still a free country," Dr. Maxie said. I must have looked uneasy, because she said, "Sis knows that."

"I guess I do too," I said, all of a sudden feeling more stand-upish.

The rest of the hour flew by. I don't remember what we talked about except when I was leaving Dr. Maxie said, "See you next week . . . and don't forget."

"I won't," I said. "Promise."

On Friday, Valentine's Day, Sis stood at four hundred and fifty.

You might have guessed she received a Valentine from every girl in the class, even one from Gordon and Rob — nobody knows that but me.

On Saturday morning I went to the Hawkinses. There was the same freaky music coming from their house when I walked up the steps. I thought maybe I'd see a sad-faced Sis, but instead the door was opened and there was Sis Hawkins upside down in the middle of the room.

"Claudia taught me how to stand on my head," she said. "It's great for writer's cramp."

We declared a holiday Saturday. Sis and Ms. Hawkins joined us for a night out. We ate Mexican food and went to see a movie about a mechanical man who had gotten his wires crossed.

"He needs a good tune-up," Sis said.

"Just like Miss Patterson," I said.

Sis stopped for a moment, and I should have known what she was thinking. "That's it," she said.

"What's it?" I said.

She just giggled.

I guess she is due a few secrets.

Miss Patterson Rips It

Sis looked pale on Monday. "Only four hundred and twenty-five to go," she said, jamming the notebook close to her chest. The Pledges made a big bunch.

The day began uneventfully. But in Language Arts, Rob accidentally tore a page in Miss Patterson's private dictionary.

Miss Patterson barked, "How dare you! That's my book!"

Rob said he was sorry, but as the morning wore on, Miss Patterson grew sourer and sourer, like Rob had done it on purpose.

Sis wrote Pledges at recess. I played.

The kids tried to wean her away, but she kept at it.

And it's funny about people. Instead of being sympathetic, the kids turned grumpy. May walked away complaining, "You're no fun."

By 1:00, the room was too warm, my stomach was full and I was sleepy. Miss Patterson was deep in the Civil War.

She stood at the blackboard and tapped the surface with her ruler, pointing out generals, troop movements and battlefields.

Tap . . . talk. Tap . . . talk. Tap . . . talk. Nap making.

I put my chin on my arms and tried to concentrate; nothing held me long. I yawned so much, I felt my teeth needed air.

I had company. Everyone was glassy-eyed. May was dozing, and for once, I wished I had fat eyelids like her. No one would know if I was asleep or awake.

The only activity from any of us was Sis writing like mad in her book.

I was counting the seconds on the classroom clock when it happened.

Blapp! A ruler hit the desk.

I sat up like I was shot.

I saw Miss Patterson leaning over Sis. Her voice was slimy, like wet soap. "You are not paying attention," she said, grabbing Sis's notebook.

"Don't," Sis pleaded, trying to hold on to her papers.

Too late.

I watched the loose sheets swish out from their binding onto the floor.

Miss Patterson's voice was deadly. "Well . . . Well . . ." she said, picking up each sheet as if it were soiled.

The class leaned forward.

"Gimme them back," Sis said, making a lunge for the papers.

Miss Patterson jerked them to her chest. "No!"

"They are mine," Sis said louder.

Miss Patterson returned to her desk with the papers; the inspection continued.

Sis tried to follow, but — I don't know why — Gordon held her back.

The room was so still, the papers flipping over sounded like crackling fire.

What can she do? I thought.

I saw she was separating the papers evenly. With one pile in each hand, she walked toward Sis and dropped one stack on her desk.

Sis automatically reached for the other.

I knew Sis had false hopes; Miss Patterson was smiling that smile of hers.

As deliberately as an executioner, she put her hands on each end of the other stack and tore it in two. Over two hundred pledges gone!

Scraddle. *Rip.*

I couldn't believe it. I sat back like my breath was just knocked out of my body. The whole class too.

It was awful.

It got worse.

Sis stood up and I watched her face twist in such pain, I wanted to run away.

She opened her mouth as if to cry, but nothing came out.

A moment passed.

Then, from some deep part of her body no one had ever seen, a strange sound arose. It was a moan of someone drowning before your eyes. Like a leaf dropping off a tree, Sis collapsed on the desk and put her head in her arms. I watched her body shake. She didn't moan again, just shook.

Miss Patterson moved so smoothly to the wastebasket, I thought she must be on rollers. The papers disappeared over the edge, and Miss Patterson clapped her hands together like she was dusting away something rotten.

I swear if I had had a gun, I would have shot her.

The class too. Now, I'm sure, the class too.

Standing Up

I thought poor, poor Polly Banks.

Can you believe it! I was watching my best friend moan like she was drowning and I was feeling sorry for myself. Then, I thought of Dr. Maxie saying, "You have to fight bravely for your rights . . . for your independence."

I didn't want to think about that, so what did I do? I tried thinking of something else like playing ball or climbing mountains.

It didn't work.

Take it from the shrink-kid, you might as well let the troublesome idea grab you and take you down its path, because it's not going away.

I squirmed and wiggled. I looked around.

Everyone else was having mixed-up thoughts, I could tell.

When the bell rang, you should have seen the class take off. You would have thought Sis was a leper. Who wants to be around a fallen champion? Falling can be contagious.

I should have been sympathetic. Didn't I know how it felt for people to run away from my stuttering? Even with Dr. Maxie's words running through my mind, I wanted to escape too.

As I walked out of the room following Sis, I thought: Didn't I try to help? Well, it's Sis's fault for being careless. What does she expect? Does she want me to get the papers out of the basket? I can't do that; I have to go home. Why do I feel so bad inside?

Sis was a mess. On the school steps she faced me and her cheeks looked like creek run-offs. She had cried so much her nose was wet like a puppy's.

I stood stiff-legged.

I couldn't talk, not the way I was feeling. She couldn't either.

At the first corner, she ran toward home, and I was glad to see her go.

My mom knew something had happened. When I tried to say hello, my stuttering was so bad I gave up and switched on the TV.

Supper was awful. When my dad said, "Got a new basketball today," I said very sarcastically, "B...B...Big d...d...deal!"

I'll give them credit; they let me alone.

I dreamed a rock had rolled down a mountain and Sis was trapped under it.

She was crying out, "Polly! Polly! Help me!"

I was trying to run away, but I couldn't. My feet were glued heading downhill.

I woke up crying. My mom was there. She just held me. She didn't make me talk.

Sis was absent the next day. Crying can make you sick. The class passed her empty chair like it was an empty grave.

May looked pale; Sarah was fidgeting, rubbing her hands together like she was having a hard time controlling herself; Gordon kept his eyes on the floor; Cynthia copied her homework three times, and the first time it was letter perfect.

Only Miss Patterson appeared untroubled. I guess she had had a good night's sleep, and a satisfying breakfast, traces of egg still clung to her chin. But she was as wound up as a rattlesnake ready to strike. She must have congratulated herself, "Now I have control."

I started coming to my senses in Language Arts.

Funny things kept running through my mind. I'd think about Dr. Maxie, then I'd think of prisons and tyrants. I thought of Belle and Otto.

I watched Miss Patterson sitting at her desk, smiling, telling me about nouns and verbs, earning her money, not bothered with Pledge-writing, not troubled with stuttering.

Then I looked around the room. My friends looked scared, like prisoners. I wouldn't have been surprised if every kid had suddenly sprouted a gray uniform with a number. Rob was shaking in his chair, May was sneaking one candy bar after another in her mouth — it was awful.

Nobody was free, not the big mature girls who looked like they were going on sixteen or the little girls like me.

Miss Patterson was turning the non-freaks into freaks right before my eyes.

I've got to tell you how it felt, me sitting there, just in case you ever have a thinking fit like I did. My feet got hot first, then my legs, my stomach. I felt the heat in my face. I'm sure I turned red; I was that mad.

I must have sat up quickly, because Miss

Patterson turned to me, me, the great stuttering freak. And you know what! I met her eyes. I, who had cried the week before because of a little embarrassment, I looked her square in the face, eyeball to eyeball, just like Sis would have done.

I knew I was getting somewhere. She looked away.

The bell rang. Recess.

Before, I'd always grabbed my coat and raced out, following Sis. That day I was too angry. I put on my coat so deliberately and walked down the steps so carefully, I thought, I'm leading a parade.

We were too mixed-up to play games. We milled around in small groups on the playing field. When I yelled, "Come over here. It's important," everyone gathered quickly.

I had their attention when I said, "It's about Sis . . ." I lit the fuse when I said, "and Miss Patterson."

A cannon went off.

"Why'd she do it?"

"I hate her."

"I hate this school."

"She should be fired."

"Sat upon," May said.

I waited a moment before I held up my hands. "What are we going to do about Sis?"

110

Silence.

"What *can* we do about her?" Rob said.

"Let's eat," May said.

"Let's play ball," two boys in the back said.

"Shut up!" Gordon yelled, stepping forward. "Let Polly talk."

I took a deep breath, because I didn't have any plans. But, suddenly (and one day I'm going to track down what happens in my head), I got an idea. Maybe it came from Dr. Maxie or from the story of Belle and Otto or maybe I just thought it up myself, but I said, "We have to strike a blow for freedom!"

(I know it sounds corny, but I was dead serious.)

"I can't hit anybody," Sarah whined.

"What do you mean?"

"Come on, let's play."

"Shut up!" Gordon said again.

"We have to get together," I paused, "and strike."

"A strike!"

"We can picket," said two girls in the back who wore bras.

"A Pledge strike!" I yelled.

It took a few moments for the idea to catch on. Mandalay has freaky kids, but they are smart.

Rob got it first. "We'll write through History."

"All day," Gordon added.

May said, "No English."

"We'll shoot Miss Patterson with . . ."

"Her own gun."

"And save Sis," I yelled.

Rob was smart, as I have said. "But what if she throws ours away?"

"We'll write more."

"And more."

"She'll give in."

"She has to."

The kids were laughing and patting each other on the back, jumping up and down like a celebration.

I had to shout to pull them back; the hair on my neck had risen — Miss Patterson was watching.

"Hold it," I said, nodding at the window.

No one said a word. Two teams formed; a kickball game started.

Our team won. "For Sis," I said, kicking a home run.

The rest of the day zipped by. Now, I answered questions trotting through my head: When would we start writing? Tomorrow. Would we tell Sis? Yes. Who would have to be watched? Sarah. Why? She's untrust-worthy. Who would be dependable? Sis, Gordon, Cynthia and me.

I got organized. (My mother would have been proud!)

After school, I met with Gordon, Rob, May and Cynthia. Gordon said he'd be sure the regular guys stayed in line; Cynthia said she'd see to all the girls who looked sixteen. (Cynthia's sister is the most popular girl in the eighth grade. The fact doesn't impress me, but it does some people.)

May said she would take care of Sarah. "If she doesn't go along, I'll sit on her," May said, adding, "Squish!"

I had to tell Sis.

I ran all the way to her house.

I don't know what I expected — Sis writing Pledges, Sis mad, Sis standing on her head. I got something different.

Ms. Hawkins met me at the door, looking like she'd lost her last Women's Lib pamphlet.

"Where's Sis," I asked.

Ms. Hawkins motioned upstairs. "She's pretty low."

I took the steps two at a time, half hearing Ms. Hawkins' "Writing Pledges can be char-acter building."

I threw open Sis's door. "Guess what?" I screamed so loud that Oliver Wendell Holmes howled once.

Nothing.

Sis's room was dark. It smelled like a hospital. Vicks Spray Mist mixed with soggy granola. The shades were pulled down tightly against the winter sun.

I could hardly see the hump in the bed. My eyes adjusted to the grayness. Sis's round face appeared from the mound of covers. She was squinched up like a small pea in a large pod. In fact she looked spring-greenish.

"Go away," she mumbled.

"Get out of bed!" I said.

"Don't wanta!" She buried her head again.

"No way!" I screamed, leaping over the footboard and bouncing on the bed. "Get up!"

She rose from her cocoon like a fired-up butterfly.

"I want to be sick," she yelled.

Squeek, squanch, the springs sang.

"Good news! Great news!" I said, bouncing high.

"I'm warning you . . ." Sis said, pulling her fist back. She was having a hard time standing up. "Get off my bed."

She struck out. Missed.

"Woopee!" I yelled. "Everything's wonderful!" Bounce. Bounce.

"I don't want to hear it!" She jabbed at me. Scrunch went the springs.

"It's about Miss Patterson . . ."

"I hate Miss Patterson," Sis said.

Bang! Her fist caught me in the eye on the top of a bounce. My feet flew up. I sailed off the bed onto the floor.

Flop!

I saw stars, and they weren't in the flag. They were on Sis's ceiling.

As Ms. Hawkins said later, "If you're going to be a general, you have to expect to get the first bullet."

Two cups of mint tea and an ice bag later, I had told the entire plan.

Sis got better and better. Ms. Hawkins was so excited she stood on her head in the kitchen.

By 4:30, Sis was dressed, and I expect she'd have sat in the classroom all night waiting for the strike if school had been open.

My eye was hurting less and less.

I was standing at the door saying goodbye, and a funny thing happened.

"Polly," Sis began. "I really . . ."

I wanted to run away.

She held my arm. "Listen to me."

I felt the switch in my throat start to click over, but for some reason it stayed in normal.

"Thank you," she said.

I barely said, "You're welcome."

I waved and ran out the door, down the driveway and did not stop until I reached home. I paused to catch my breath before I dashed through the house, into the kitchen. My mom and dad were sitting at the table, frowning.

They had no chance to ask anything; I had so much to say.

From Pledge-tearing to striking, from me being organized to Sis's one-day nervous breakdown, my story kept coming. When I ended with, "Look at my eye!" it was an anticlimax.

My dad leaned back and said, "Start over and tell it again."

I did.

Rounding Up Miss Patterson

When I woke up on February 19, the day of the strike, the air was exciting, like Christmas. For example, you know your presents are under the tree, but you move slowly as if you were putting off some pleasure yet hurting to get it over with.

That's how I felt. It was a big event, and I wanted to look well-organized. I put on my best sweater and skirt, white knee socks, and I even polished my shoes.

I looked serious even with my black eye.

When I got to school, the class was gathered around the flagpole. It was still cold. Everyone was stamping his feet; steamy breath hung in the icy air. They reminded me

117

of a western movie, of horses getting ready for a round-up.

Sis stood outside the group. Gordon was talking. "Sit down and start writing after the roll call," he said. "Nobody stop. Not if she calls your name or threatens you . . . You understand?" He gave one of his hairy looks to the three boys who never follow directions. "If you don't . . ." Gordon continued, I'm going to . . ." — something I can't put down; Gordon is a leader, but he uses ripe language.

Cynthia gave it to the girls. May whispered something in Sarah's ear which made her shake like a tree in a high wind.

When the bell rang, we lined up quickly and silently.

I saw a real old movie once of a queen about to have her head cut off. I remember how brave she appeared being driven to the guillotine.

That's how we looked, brave but underneath terrified.

Once inside, we knew there was no going back.

The roll call seemed endless.

The book shut. Miss Patterson stood up, her chair scraped away from her desk, and she walked to the back of the room.

During her usual meditation, we had time.

Usually it was quiet but not today.

Eyes met eyes. Then, spreading like a brush fire, note pads appeared: yellow pencils flashed.

Crackle . . . scribble.

When Miss Patterson turned around she could only have seen backs bent over paper.

I pledge allegiance . . .

I don't know why I glanced at the picture of George Washington over the flag. I think he was smiling.

Since Rob had said, "Don't look up," I can only tell what I heard.

First, over the scraping of pencils, Miss Patterson squeaked, "What are you doing?"

Nobody answered.

She clapped her hands together. "Order! Order!"

No change.

She stepped briskly to the front of the room and banged her ruler on the desk. "Children, the Pledge!"

She didn't know, but we were doing the Pledge!

Again silence.

Her voice rose. I had started on my second Pledge when she called, "May!" No answer. "Rob! Gordon!"

Only scribbling.

She paced up and down behind the desks, hitting the ruler in her palm. Step . . . slap. Step . . . slap. Step . . . slap.

I thought of a ruler guillotine.

"Harrumph," she said.

I braced myself for the ruler in the neck, but she started on Sarah Coots. It was so dirty, I got madder. The other kids too, I am sure.

I watched Sarah out of the corner of my eye so I know what was happening. Miss Patterson bent over Sarah's desk and said in her most cutesy-cutesy voice, "Sarah, dear, you know you don't want to be a part of this silly little game, now do you?" She took a breath. "After all," she said, pausing, searching for the right words. I think she was going to say, "Too rich," instead she said, "Too pretty."

I watched Sarah shake herself as if a snake had touched her. Then, without looking at May or anybody, she continued to write faster.

Miss Patterson tried everyone from Gordon and Cynthia to two girls who sometimes washed her blackboard during recess. (They hated sports.) She tried to appeal to the boy who cleaned her erasers. (I've seen him skip behind the school and smoke.)

Nobody gave up writing.

I was on my sixth Pledge.

"I'm getting Miss Heartbang," Miss Patterson announced.

Footsteps over the floor. Door opened. Shut. Miss Patterson returned to her desk.

One more Pledge.

Silence.

"Stop it!"

Nothing.

"I'm going to call your parents."

Footsteps over the floor. Door opened. Shut. Miss Patterson returned to her desk.

The clock struck 10:00. The recess bell rang. We all walked out of the room.

It was a great relief; my hand felt like it was dead.

When we got outside, we had a celebration. Everyone congratulated Sarah. She beamed.

Only Rob was cautious. "Patterson has other ammunition," he said.

When recess was over we headed back. There on the board in chalk was the Pledge written in Miss Patterson's grade three script. An I've-got-you-now smile decorated her face.

"Copy one hundred times," she said.

I heard a pencil drop. Sis was leaning back with her arms crossed.

Gordon sat back. Rob followed. The eraser-cleaner put his pencil down.

Have you ever had the elastic break in your pants? They slip off so gradually you don't realize what's happening until they are around your ankles.

That was how Miss Patterson looked when everyone folded his arms and sat back; her face elastic broke. Her forehead slipped; her eyes got dull; her smile just fell around her ankles.

And at that moment, I felt sorry for her. She was a hurt person then.

It's too bad she had a twenty-gun temper tantrum.

She roared up and down the aisles yelling and screaming. She put on her Southern Heritage act. We were unpatriotic. We were traitors. On and on . . .

When the lunch bell rang, she had run down.

The class left quietly. Miss Patterson was sitting looking out the window.

Sis and I hung back as the class walked down the steps to the lunchroom. There was no excitement now. Sis and I looked at each other. We knew what we had to do.

Sis said, "Let's go."

We went to Miss Heartbang's office. She was alone.

It took fifteen minutes to tell what happened. Sis can really shrink down a story.

"Oh, my!" Miss Heartbang said three times. Then, "Oh, dear, poor children. Poor Miss Patterson. I'd better get Miss Tillstrom."

She left the room and Sis and I watched Miss Patterson being gently led to her car.

When she and Miss Tillstrom drove off, I felt things were under better control. Miss Patterson would not be alone.

Nobody Hides For Long

After we got back in the room, Miss Heartbang took over. She said nothing about Miss Patterson.

We were all high when school was out. Everyone wanted to keep together. So Sis, May, Sarah, Rob — Cynthia had to attend Hebrew class; Gordon had basketball practice — we began talking and walking. We stopped every two blocks to retell a part of the story.

I don't know how we got to my house. Gangs of kids had never gathered there before, but we trooped in.

My mom and Ms. Hawkins were sitting in the kitchen. As they listened to the whole thing, I could see they were worried.

Only when I said we'd told Miss Heartbang the whole story and Miss Tillstrom had taken charge of Miss Patterson did they relax.

My mom said, "Maybe this is her chance to do some real thinking."

"This calls for a celebration," Ms. Hawkins said.

My mom got busy serving apple juice and cookies.

We were having too much fun for my mom and me to realize it was Wednesday and Wednesday was shrink day. Dr. Maxie was the last thing on my mind when the phone rang in the kitchen.

The room was still as my mom went to answer it.

"Hello," she said.

Silence.

"Oh, I'm so sorry . . . I know we did it again . . ." she stammered. (My organized mom thinks keeping your word is next to cleanliness.)

She hung up and her voice sailed over the quiet kitchen as fast as hot grease.

"Polly," she said. "We forgot your psychiatrist again."

My secret was out.

That minute must have had a thousand

seconds, because slowly Sarah's beady eyes, May's fat eyes, Rob's sad eyes focused on me.

I know now how a germ must feel under a microscope.

May, Sarah and Rob squirmed uncomfortably in their seats. I was too stunned to ask why, but Sis, old good-friend Hawkins, saved the day.

(Later, she said she took a chance, but the odds looked good.)

She cocked her head and looked at May. "What shrink do you go to?" she said.

May sighed. "Dr. Caldron."

Then, as if a great pressure had been lifted, Rob said, "I go to Dr. Proofrock."

Sarah was the last to confess. "I do too."

That was that.

Sis said later that nobody has as much in common as people who go to shrinks. She is correct, because right before my ears, the conversation lifted.

"My shrink says . . ." May began.

"Well, mine says . . ."

I even got up the nerve to say, "Dr. Maxie takes me for walks in the woods."

Sis nudged me in the shins. "My dad would have done that," she said.

"Your dad . . ." I began. Then, I knew. "Your dad was a shrink!"

She looked relieved. "Yes," she said.

"Join the group," May said.

Nobody hides for long in the world.

Miss Patterson Begins Skrinking

Miss Patterson called in sick the rest of the week; Miss Heartbang took over. She gave us a lecture on responsibility which made all of us feel uneasy.

"Of course," she said, "it's something you learn by experience."

When she added sadly, "Even adults can be confused," I felt better. She was talking about Miss Patterson.

(Miss Patterson deserves some credit. She may have been freaky, but, except for history, she never bored you to death. Miss Heartbang was as dull as insomnia.)

The week passed. On Monday, February 24, when I arrived in class, all the Southern stuff was gone. Only the American flag and

128

the picture of George Washington were left. The room looked bare.

"Miss Holmes will be in charge of you in the morning, and I will take over in the afternoon," Miss Heartbang said. "Miss Patterson will be helping me in the office."

I saw Miss Patterson as I headed down the hall for recess. She looked more at home in the office, I thought. Everything was so orderly.

At least that's what I told Dr. Maxie on Wednesday, along with all the other things that had happened. It was funny. She said exactly what my mom had said, "I think it's time she did some real thinking."

After that day, things in my life gradually got better. I still went to Dr. Maxie every week, but it was more relaxed.

Once, she said, "Life is straightening you out. You are meeting every challenge."

Even Miss Patterson faded from my mind as spring came . . . but not from Sis's.

Sis would walk away from the office having delivered the attendance report and look like one of the Governors of Georgia.

"I have to do something," she would mutter.

April came. We played in the creek until

the snakes scared us away, then we lounged under the trees, because it was too hot for games.

Sis, May, Sarah, Cynthia, and I made a good talking group.

When Sis decided we needed a class picnic, Sarah was put in charge of the money, May the food, and I got to organize the games.

I was growing more and more like my mom in some ways.

Speaking of my mom, Ms. Hawkins and she were seeing each other every other day. My dad said they must be getting into a rock polisher and rubbing off on each other, because my mom was growing a little messy while Sis said her mom was tidying up.

April flew by.

The picnic was on the first Monday in May. It was super. Sarah accounted for all the money. May's food was deliciously low-calorie — we had the only picnic I know starring cottage cheese and carrot sticks. Sis helped me organize the games and we didn't have a spare moment.

But, in the midst of kickball, Sis grew serious. I went to her side; she was gazing up. There stood Miss Patterson on top of the gravelly bank, peering down on the fun as if there was a glass wall between her and us.

Sis made up her mind then. "You know," she began, "I think that woman needs help."

I thought I knew what she meant. "Real help?"

"Walking in the woods help," Sis said.

We spent a whole afternoon on the letter.

I wanted it to be anonymous, but Sis said you had to stand by what you say. She wouldn't even let me mail it.

The last day of school when everybody was running fast away from Mandalay, Sis and I went to the office.

Miss Patterson was bent over a paper carton packing away the leftover forms and report cards.

The windows were open, and the sunlight drifted in.

Sis cleared her throat. "Miss Patterson," she said.

Miss Patterson jumped like a bee had stung her. She straightened up like her old self. "You wanted me?" she said.

I was carrying the letter, and I could feel my hands grow wet on the envelope. "We came . . ." I began.

"To say . . ." For once, Sis was speechless.

Miss Patterson had cocked her head in a funny fashion as if to say, after all you've done, what now?

"We came to say," Sis began again, "you were a good Language Arts teacher."

"Fair as a ruler over math," I said limply.

Miss Patterson still looked puzzled, then she sniffed like she had a case of hay fever. "I tried," she said.

I thrust the letter in her hand.

We stood silently as Miss Patterson turned the envelope over slowly.

I started for the door. I stopped. Miss Patterson did a funny thing. She smiled nicely. Her voice was low. "Sis, I guess I shouldn't have made you write those Pledges."

Sis shrugged her shoulders. "It's all right now."

"Come on," I said, pulling her to the door.

But Sis wasn't through. "See you next year," she called.

We were outside in a jiffy. But at the flagpole, I felt the Patterson prick on the back of my neck. I nudged Sis.

There was Miss Patterson, at the window. She was waving at us.

We waved back.

What else!

The End Really

What's happened to everyone?

Miss Patterson: After we delivered the letter with the names of three shrinks plus telephone numbers (of course they came from our mini-therapy group), summertime put Miss Patterson out of my mind. But in July, Sis said she saw Miss Patterson outside a small building with a red door surrounded by a shady woods. She was with Miss Tillstrom, and they were walking fast up the brick steps. I knew it was where Dr. Maxie shrinks.

Maybe she will turn out happy like me.

Otto Frink: My dad hired him. He now designs plastic money that is used in paperweights. Transparent Cash, it's called. He did the dollar bill, the five-dollar bill, and with inflation, he will have a full-time job.

Belle has joined NOW, and spends much of her time down at the Capitol. Sis says she's lobbying against form letters.

Ms. Hawkins: She went hiking with us and Sis this past August on my mountain in Seattle. She wore regular clothes and didn't scare a single animal.

"This is quite a trip!" she said.

She has enrolled in law school and has already organized a study-discussion-group-yoga thing.

Men look strange on their heads.

My mom and dad: We bought the house, and we are going to stay here forever, I hope. My dad is Executive Vice-President.

My mom says she is going to get a job, but I think she enjoys organizing our kitchen too much to leave.

Dr. Maxie: I stopped going to see her at the end of school. We had about covered everything I could think of. I think she was ready for me to move on, too.

The last day I stuttered so badly, she had to get out the Kleenex. I knew it was only because it was hard for me to say, "I'm really going to miss you."

At the door she said, "I'll always be here if you need me," adding gently, "but I don't think you will. No, Polly Banks, I think you've about climbed that mountain of yours."

I shook her hand and that was that.

Sis Hawkins: She's the same.

But I think she has a case on Gordon. At least she hangs around the football field a lot so she doesn't have much time for shooting baskets like we used to. Just the other day I heard her giggle like the big girls.

"Stop that!" I said.

"Try and make me," she said.

We had a great big fight, so I guess we are still best friends.

My stuttering: I still stutter off and on.

Dr. Maxie taught me a lot. I know now when I stutter it means either I'm not feeling too good about myself or I am afraid to speak up.

So, when I stutter, I watch out.

For example, the other day my mom was braiding my hair too tight.

I started stuttering, "St...St...St..."

I stopped, trying to ignore the old hurt look on my mom's face. I knew what was bothering me. I took a deep breath and looked my mom right in the eyes. "Stop that!" I said. "I don't like my hair so tight." I paused. "In fact, I don't like braids at all. I want to cut them off."

"But Polly, I like . . ." my mother began. Then she paused, shrugged her shoulders and said, "OK, Toots, I'll get the scissors."

Dr. Maxie was right; you have to fight for your rights, especially the rights of your hair.

Me: I'm changing like Sis. Just yesterday I talked to my mom about wearing more than undershirts.

"You're not a little girl anymore," my mom said.

I started to say, "Rats!" Then I thought, why not? What's wrong with a little maturity?

Things look pretty good ahead.

I'll let you know if they aren't.